Troubled Waters Presents:

A Different

Type of Enemy

by Rashad M. Riddick

Troubled Waters Publishing
P.O. Box 4030
Petersburg, VA 23803

ISBN: 978-0-692-09569-0

"*Outside Kandahar, 27 war-hungry American soldiers took two teenage girls back to their camp. For three weeks, they tortured, gang raped and abused the girls as if they were nothing. Later, a local preacher in the village where the girls were kidnapped, who also ran his own religious school, went to the army camp with 30 students and 16 rifles. Against all odds, they overwhelmed the American Soldiers and hung the Commander of the unit from the barrel of a tank gun. The priest's name was Mohammad Omar, or Mullah Omar. He lost his right eye in the battle. The news spread. Others appealed to him for help. He and his group swelled in numbers. They took no money, they raped no women, they stole no crops, they asked no reward for their undertakings. They eventually became local heroes. By December 1994, twelve thousand had joined them, adopting the mullahs black turban. They called themselves 'The Students'. In Pashto, 'Talib' means student. In* plural, 'Taliban'. From village vigilantes, they became a full blown movement. And, after capturing the city of Kandahar, they became an alternative government."

Ibn Hamzah al-Zukari

Prologue

"Thank you sir. As I was saying, these men have not been linked to any deaths whatsoever in which children or anyone else for that matter were killed. In fact, a thorough investigation has held that these men not only govern and shield the inner city youth from what some may call the "Powers That Be", but they are known for establishing programs specifically designed to *help* troubled youth."

The black baldheaded man in the backseat of the navy blue Grand Marquise paused to scratch his nose before continuing.

"And the fact that none of this is on official record says a lot. They do what they do because they love doing it. These men aren't for show.

They don't do things for recognition. These men earn their respect in the community by their true and genuine actions on a daily basis."

The two men in the front seat listened intently. Agent Crawford and Agent Davis were part of a joint FBI/CIA/NSA task force. Agent Davis was NSA. Agent Crawford was CIA.

They were currently tracking and investigating a group of men that they felt were violent and responsible for a large number of high profile deaths of political figures. Senators. Police. Delegates. You name it.

From a legal standpoint, the CIA was not supposed to mess with United States citizens. They were a spy agency specifically designed to protect Americans from threats abroad.

But what got the CIA involved, and made the task force quasi-legal, was an allegation that these men were from Kazakhstan.

For this reason alone they had been labeled terrorists and deemed a threat to national security. Natuarally NSA and CIA got involved as a result.

But the thought never crossed any of their minds for a split second that "The Brotherhood" itself, as the joint task force so often called them during briefing, may itself be the target of a complex conspiracy.

All of the joint task forces clandestine meetings at Federal Headquarters were all one sided and showed everything in a negative light regarding The Brotherhood. Yet, neither of the agencies *ever* found one shred of real evidence of illegal activity on the part of the individuals they painted as being monsters.

Only suspicions.

Additionally, The Brotherhood was invisible from a surveillance standpoint. None of the alleged members had a Facebook page. None of them had flashy cars. None of them sped while they were driving. None of them ran red lights.

This bothered both the FBI and the CIA in the worse way.

Most African American movements and organized crime figures in the inner city were flamboyant and only hoped to be feared and recognized by other knuckleheads and underworld crime figures.

Not these men.

Whoever led them made sure that they had no *known* structure.

Crawford glanced into the rearview mirror. The face of the black baldheaded man who briefed them about The Brotherhood was without expression. He seemed to be in a deep trance-like state of mind when talking… as if he didn't have a soul. Crawford broke him out of it.

"Uh, Mr. Simms? Mr. Simms is your name right?"

"Yes that's correct sir" The black baldheaded responded.

"Okay Mr. Simms. Now exactly how much information do you have on The Brotherhood? From what I'm hearing, it seems like you are making a sort of, uhhh…sort of, well… justification in regards to these men. Now me and my partner here have direct orders to kill two men who are the alleged leaders and masterminds of this organization. Do you really and truly believe that there is some sort of conspiracy in the government trying to frame *these* two assholes?"

The baldheaded man slowly took his glasses off and folded them into his breast pockets before answering.

"No sir. I *know*."

Agent Crawford exploded.

"You black baldheaded mutherfucker you listen to me! You sit here and…"

Boom!! Boom!! Boom!! Boom!! Boom!!

The black baldheaded man in the back seat emptied 5 large hollow-point slugs from a .40

caliber semi-automatic handgun into the right side of Agent Crawford's head.

The front dashboard and windshield had small fragments of flesh and what appeared to be a chunk of Agent Crawford's mustache.

Agent Davis froze in shock. His instincts as a seasoned NSA agent didn't kick in at all.

In fact, reaching for the gun in his waistband didn't even cross his mind. The bitch in him kicked in.

The black baldheaded man in the back seat shook his head in disgust. Not at the brain matter on the front windshield, but how police and other calibers of law enforcement were always the ones delivering blows   and effecting arrests and surprise attacks in the wee hours of the morning while a man slept with his family. They were cocky as hell in numbers. In fact the shit seemed to be funny to them to see a black man scared out of their wits after suddenly being awakened out of their sleep to 25 white men with assault-style rifles and bullet proof vests screaming "get on the ground".

Yet when shit got real, they were cowards in the worse sense.

The black baldheaded man peered at t Agent Davis through the rearview mirror from the back seat. He still sat calmly as if he did not just blow a man's brains out or smell the strong scent of graphite and burning flesh in the vehicle.

"Sir? Mr. Davis?" The black baldheaded tried to get Agent Davis' attention.

Agent Davis' ears were still ringing from the loud blasts that had just rang out in the small space. It had been a full 30 seconds since the shots rang out, but all of Agent Davis' faculties had ceased to function properly and he could not hear anything.

"Hey mutherfucker do you hear me? Do you feel the same way that your partner right there feels?"

The baldheaded man talked about the dead Agent as if he were still alive.

"No. No. Hell no." Came the reply from Agent Davis.

"Very well then."

The baldheaded man put the gun back onto his waistband nonchalantly and scratched his head with a yawn.

He spoke again.

"Now, let me reintroduce myself by my *honorable* name. My name is Brother Haleef. The guys that you and your partner speak of are my brothers…"

Suddenly, a long muffled sound was heard throughout the vehicle followed by a foul stench. Agent Davis had shitted himself.

"Now Mr. Davis, I have your daughter at my house playing video games with my son. She is really enjoying herself."

A tear fell down Agent Davis face.

But brother Haleef had more to say.

"She is very beautiful too. Now, I told my son to be nice to her and that she was only staying for the weekend and that her father had to go out of town in a hurry."

Brother Haleef began cleaning his fingernails during the brief pause as if the cuticle on his fingers were more important than what was going on at the moment.

"If you so much as utter a word about what just occurred, I will make sure that my son has a field day with her. He is 13 and he is most definitely willing to engage with your 11 year old daughter."

He wasn't bluffing.

"Your new assignment is to convince your little joint task force that Agent Crawford went rouge and is responsible for setting my brothers up."

Brother Haleef looked out the window nonchalantly.

"You are to make it appear that he left the country and feared that he would be exposed. I don't care how you do it or who you have to get involved. You just better trust them with your daughter's life to keep all of this our little secret."

The black baldheaded man began to open the door and get out but stopped short.

"And please clean this shit up."

Chapter 1

Haleef got out of the unmarked car and casually walked down Warwick Boulevard. He had just killed a C.I.A agent, yet he walked down the street whistling and playing with his fingernails.

He had not a worry in the word. And if anyone had any knowledge whatsoever of the things that Haleef had been through, he had died a long time ago. At least psychologically.

And what was one more dead C.I.A agent when hundreds had been killed over the years in foreign wars in other countries. They didn't even have tombstones or a marked grave for their services.

In fact, they were known to have simply been left in the street dying. The stated purpose was that in their line of work, what they did was so sensitive, they had to fend for themselves if captured or hurt in any way.

Or better put, what they did was patently illegal and the United States did not want to be connected with any illegal activity whatsoever.

But let America tell it, they were the saviors of the international community that could do no wrong.

Most people had no idea that America had essentially started every single war in the modern world since the 60's.

Haleef had been AWOL, wanted for murdering an American soldier and shown on Americas Most Wanted nearly 53 times in the past 4 years.

It was no use though. Haleef had 4 facial reconstructions in the past 7 years. America had a way of catching up with one changing their identity. The satellites nowadays had the capacity to detect your height and gait. This was how you walked, the distance of your steps, your manner of walk, your posture, and your pace.

So not only did Haleef have to change his physical appearance, he spent many nights altering his walk. One day he would feign a limp. Another day he slightly dragged his feet. He walked slew footed. Pigeon toed. Whatever came to mind that day and depending on where he was in relation to each satellite.

An old friend of Haleef's whom was a naval intelligence officer in the late 90's had shown him a space map of all known U.S. satellites.

There were 847 U.S satellites hovering over North America alone. Of these, 129 were used to spy on Americans in the worst way. They could see you in real time. They penetrated through your home via heat emissions from your body and x-ray technology.

These satellites had capabilities that should shock the conscience of any American as most satellites can record and decipher every word and vibration coming from a human beings mouth. They often detected vibrations so faint, that it would decipher a whispered conversation with the clarity of a recorded song in the studio.

But Haleef didn't care. As long as he knew what capabilities the U.S government had, he could go undetected right here in America for the rest of his life.

Haleef had gotten a call from his nephew Wyreek last week. They had been in constant contact over the years and not a soul knew about it. Not even Amir, his best friend. It had to be that way.

Both Haleef and Wyreek knew that if Haleef's whereabouts were ever known by the American government he would be killed by one of America's elite Black Ops Units without a trial.

And now his own nephew had gone into hiding after a paid hit he and Amir chose to partake in for $8 million.

Wyreek's contact said that he and Amir were hired to complete the assignment specifically due to their closeness to the individuals involved. Both Wyreek and Amir brought a number of very important people together for fundraising events, and sit-downs with gang leaders nationwide. And honestly, the support only came because gangs threatened the families and pockets of rich and powerful people.

But Wyreek and Amir were particularly close to one of these individuals. Senator Ted Collinwood.

Senator Ted Collinwood had actually been the one that set up the *invites* for fundraising events. But he was hated by longtime political figures. This was because his proposals for legislation as well as the many things that he had done throughout the country were for the African American community.

At first Wyreek and Amir refused the assignment. They could not see themselves killing a man that did so much for their community.

Then, one day, a DVD was sent to both Wyreek and Amir's home. It was a recording of Wyreek, Amir, two Senators, a presidential candidate and four billionaires discussing openly a plan to essentially overthrow the United States government.

It was recorded in Ted Collinwood's condominium. A loft that had been bugged for many years by the Central Intelligence Agency.

The content on the tape itself was enough to have all of those on the tape on trial for treason.

And though the recording was illegally obtained and the CIA is not supposed to spy on American citizens, there were ways to get it in court. The Patriot Act.

After 9/11, the United States Constitution had essentially become null and void. There was absolutely nothing that the American government could not do. This included spying on its own senators, judges, congressman and even the president himself.

No one was exempt from espionage.

Wyreek had continuously replayed in his head the recorded meeting, the shooting, his loyalty to his brothers, and this whole speech by his contact who ordered the killings who stated that it was all for the *greater good* of the people.

Wyreek came to the conclusion that he had been set up by the American government.

He needed his uncle's advice and guidance.

Wyreek saw the number 16 bus come into view. It was right on time. 10:00 a.m. on the dot. Well, it was 10:03 a.m. but you couldn't get any more precise than that.

Wyreek had not ridden the bus since he was 14 years old. But he had been directed to by his uncle.

Haleef inserted his money into the machine and sat down. He then pulled out his cell phone and dialed his uncle.

"Unk, I'm on the Ten O'clock"

Chapter 2

Haleef felt the vibration of his phone and reached into his pocket to answer it.

It was Wyreek.

Haleef was proud of his nephew. He was a great listener.

Haleef had directed Wyreek to get on the 10:00 a.m. number 16 bus which would arrive at exactly 10:03 a.m.

Haleef further directed Wyreek that if Unk did not get on the bus at the Thorncliff Drive bus stop scheduled for pick up at 10:39 a.m., to get off the bus, go directly behind the Food Lion and kill the two individuals in the navy blue Grand Marquise.

But thank God that it never came to that.

Chapter 3

"What's wrong 'Amir'?" A pleasant female voice with a heavy Jamaican accent echoed in the small kitchen.

"Aint shit baby girl, I'm just waiting on Reek to get back at me. It's like 4 in the morning and I haven't heard anything from my lil' nigga since we left that house party on 29th street."

Amir responded as he paced the kitchen. It was always like him to be paranoid, but not like this.

The female voice spoke again.

"Did you call his Aunt Brenda's house yet? You know he fixed up her basement a few weeks ago."

"Yeah, I called there first."

Wyreek, known in the streets as "Lil' Rico" and "Reek" for short, was Amir's other half. The two of them could damn near predict each other's next move. So if one of them did not know where the other was, it was serious.

The voice in the kitchen was that of his wife and best friend Medina sensing the tension of her man and her mind springing into action. She hated when Amir went through things alone.

Medina remembered a sudden phone call they got earlier in the day from a guy that Amir dealt with on and off named Roscoe. The phone had stopped ringing by the time she got to it but she saw the number on the caller ID and took note of it.

"I think Roscoe was trying to get in touch with you earlier baby. The phone in the basement only rang twice so I couldn't grab it in time. Did you ever get up with him?" Medina asked as she walked towards the huge oak cabinet in the living room and poured two shots of Hennessey.

"Nah but I saw his nephew at the gas station when I went to pick up some blunts before the party."

Amir could only think the worse. The way things were going for the past few months there wasn't any telling why Wyreek had not gotten back at him and was not able to be reached.

"Roscoe." He thought to himself. Why in the fuck was he calling? He owed 'Amir' money.

Niggas who owe money don't call people that they owe money to. And why would he call the house phone if he had both cell phone numbers?

Amir thought about something.

"Medina I need you to handle something for me baby girl."

Medina was already walking towards Amir with the drinks in her hand. Whenever he needed her to handle something she felt that roller-coaster feeling deep down inside for some reason.

And it wasn't fear, it was excitement. It was the thought of all of the things that they had been through over the years. This is what she lived for.

Amir smiled at Medina, the two of them had been married for four years. She was still the most beautiful woman in the world to him. He stared into her eyes and wondered if maybe she could read his mind at times.

They were like Pinky & The Brain. Except neither of them were the Pinky sort. They were both 'Brain's'. Leaders.

"Medina, I need you to meet up with Wyreek's girlfriend. It's too early in the morning right now but as soon as you think that she might be up, I want the both of you to go shopping and relax a little. At least appear to. Just to get the feel of her and see if she is acting differently."

Medina squinted her eyes at him as they both downed the two straight shots of Hennessey. She couldn't stand Wyreek's girlfriend.

Ever since they were in High School Medina had a real funny feeling about Nikiriya.

Amir continued on.

"When you meet up with her, I want you to squeeze everything you can out of that bitch. She should have been the first chicken to cluck if something was wrong with Wyreek."

There was a long silence as Amir split open a White Owl cigar with his fingernail. Rolling a blunt to him was like yoga meditation. It calmed him. It made him relax.

About 30 seconds after rolling the blunt he lit it at the end and took a deep drag of the reefer before addressing Medina.

"I called Nikki's cell phone around 2:00 this morning and she didn't sound too surprised at all that Wyreek was AWOL. That being said, I need you to wrinkle her shirt up a little bit."

Amir gave Medina a devilish grin.

"Just don't hurt the bitch Medina. Fuck her up most definitely. But just don't hurt her."

Medina couldn't wait to see Nikiriya now. The burn from the Hennessy she just swallowed was nothing. The only thing that ran through her mind was finding out what was going on for her king.

"Did you put the rest of the squad on point yet?" Medina asked after a brief silence.

"Nah I need to see what's up before I put them niggas on alert. Once they go on the move I can't stop them."

This was the dangerous part about having goons that are loyal. Once you give them the word it's already done. There is no such thing as 'hold up wait, nah, just give it a minute.'

In fact, he had specifically instructed them to change their numbers and not call him or anyone else until whatever was asked of them had been completed.

And as it related to accuracy, dedication and commitment, whenever called upon Amir could direct each and every one his brothers into a cave full of snakes blindfolded and not one of them would get bitten.

So shit could really get out of hand unnecessarily if it was a false alarm and he was merely being paranoid.

A million thoughts popped into Amir's head. What if Wyreek is dead? What if the people they were ordered to kill last Thursday was a set up to get him and his best friend Wyreek out of the way?

Medina glanced over at Amir. She could see that he was stressing.

"Come here baby." Medina moved closer to Amir and straddled him so that they were sitting face to face.

Medina massaged his shoulders while still facing him.

Only after about 5 minutes did Amir began to open up a little.

"I apologize for not telling you what me and Wyreek had going on a lot sooner baby."

Medina didn't know where he was going with this, but she planned to listen to anything Amir had to say and wait for instructions.

"Medina, me and Wyreek got into some shit a few nights ago. We made a quick run to Memphis to handle a small situation that turned out to be a lot bigger than we expected. To keep it brief, a few important people got killed."

Medina couldn't believe that Amir was holding things back from her. But she still kept quiet and did not interrupt his thought process.

Amir broke eye contact with Medina. He knew he had fucked up. He did not want to destroy their trust, but it was just some things that could not be told in full.

Sensing his wife's apprehension he addressed it.

"I know baby girl and I apologize again. I should have put you on point."

He took a deep drag of the reefer and handed it to Medina before continuing on.

"We were given an assignment baby."

Medina knew this to mean a paid hit. A murder for hire.

Gently, Amir brushed a strand of hair from Medina's face with his thumb.

"But that's not even what's bothering me. The shit that is bothering me is that none of it even made the news baby."

Amir shook his head slightly and appeared to be removing a number of images from his head.

"They will air a missing dog on the 5:00 o'clock and 6:00 o'clock news, and list a bunch of cornball niggas with probation violations and parking tickets, but not a shootout in broad daylight in front of a bunch of white kids? Nah, this shit is crazy baby. We were shooting for like 6 minutes straight out there. That shit should have been on CNN."

Medina's head was spinning. She remembered the look on Amir and Wyreek's faces at the bowling alley on Thursday night. They were always getting into shit. She figured it was just another day.

But Medina always had the gut feeling that Amir and Wyreek both had a lot going on in the streets.

Not too long ago, Medina had attended a fundraising event with Amir and Wyreek.

Everywhere she looked there were a bunch of white folks addressing each other as 'Mr. Senator' this 'Mr. Congressman' that.

But as soon as Amir and Wyreek walked into the room, these same white men were asking Amir and Wyreek to take photos with them and breaking their necks to shake hands like they were Gods.

She knew Amir was a powerful man by how he moved in the streets and how people interacted with him. His associations alone blew her mind.

But strangely, this power and fear that he had over others that she had seen with her own eyes made her pussy wet. In fact, this is what drew her to him in the first place.

Everybody else perceived him to be dangerous. Not Medina. She felt that he was just handling whatever came at him. He just needed the right woman in his life and to be loved.

Nevertheless, Amir never told her anything. She guessed that this is what he preferred so that she could maintain her sanity.

Medina knew from reading books about the Mafia and organized crime how these powerful men and women operated if shit got real. If they wanted to get at Amir they would not hesitate for one second to come for her to get at him.

This was every man's weakness. Once your enemy is aware of your woman or what you tend to love more than yourself, they will naturally use every tactic in the book to destroy it. Kids. Wife. Car. Pet Goldfish. It didn't matter.

But as a woman, and a very intelligent woman at that, Medina knew better than to enquire about matters that had nothing to do with her. Yes, it bothered her that Amir kept things from her, but Amir had been paranoid his entire life. This is how he had survived for so long.

Medina placed the blunt in the ashtray and began to twist one of Amir's dreads. It was times like this that she wished everything would stop so that they could be in each other's arms forever.

Amir suddenly started laughing.

"Baby I'm sorry. I'm tripping. I know better. I'm so used to seeing shit from the worse possible angle, I never stopped to think that maybe Wyreek has not contacted me for a reason. Shit, come to think of it we always distance ourselves after an assignment in case we are being set up or followed."

A Different Type of Enemy   **Rashad M. Riddick**

Amir leaned over and kissed Medina on her lips.

"And plus real niggas don't die. They just fade away."

Chapter 4

"Turn left up here Medina." Amir's mouth was full of food as he directed Medina from the passenger seat of the burgundy Ford Excursion. On Amir's lap was a large Tupperware full of turkey sausage, fried eggs, fried potatoes, pancakes, and what looked like a full gallon of syrup.

"That shit is good aint it?" Medina said. It was more of a statement than a question. She had made it herself.

"Hell yeah. Make another left up here baby. Stop in front of that curb by the dumpster."

How Medina had heard a single word Amir said from his mouth must have been her psychic sense, because Amir's mouth was completely filled with fried potatoes and turkey sausage.

Ten seconds later the burgundy SUV came to a complete stop in front of a blue dumpster. An older African American man in a navy blue Polo sweat suit approached the passenger side of the Excursion smoking a Black & Mild cigar.

"Peace God" The older man greeted Amir.

"Peace Allah" Amir saluted back.

The older man who approached the vehicle was known only as "The Elder."

He conversed with Amir without even looking at him directly. He was paying attention to his immediate surroundings.

"I spoke to Wyreek like 45 minutes ago. He said that everything is everything but he is not fucking with the phones."

Medina listened quietly from the driver's seat and was relieved to hear that The Elder had made contact with Wyreek. Now she did not have to meet up with that grimy bitch Nikiriya.

The Elder continued.

"He will reach out to you a little later but he's aiight though."

The Elder continued to casually look around while he spoke to Amir. His eyes suddenly landed on a white Crown Victoria sitting on the corner. It was most definitely the feds. He didn't give a fuck though.

The Elder wasn't tripping though. He knew that if the feds tried to fuck with him at this very moment his young boys sat on a porch less than 20 yards away with AK-47's on their laps watching intently. They were trained to kill and eliminate any and all threats to The Elder.

Had the unmarked vehicle moved just one inch in the direction of their mentor, two hundred 7.62 rounds would have ripped it into shreds.

While still conversing, The Elder nonchalantly dropped a small folded sheet of notebook paper into Amir's lap without warning.

The Elder never spoke on the phone. Ever. Folded sheets of notebook paper was how he communicated his more sinister thoughts. He felt that everything in modern society was bugged and wiretapped. And these were facts. So anything outside of normal chit-chat was written in a numerical code that only he and Amir could decipher.

After another quick nod from the two men, Medina put the truck in drive and slowly pulled away from the curb.

Chapter 5

Wyreek had been following NSA agents, CIA agents, Newport News Police Officers, U.S Marshals, and DEA agents for about 4 days now.

He was ordered by his uncle to not make any contact with Amir. Wyreek did not quite understand why but he did not ask any questions. If his uncle gave him the order to not contact Amir he would comply.

His uncle, Haleef, better known as The Baldheaded Man by those who did not know him or his identity, was an Ex-Special forces turned rogue.

He had been sent to Kuwait in the early nineties but never returned *officially*.

47

While there, he had seen so much corruption and cowardice in the military, he could no longer take it.

And this did not happen overnight. What struck a nerve and what he considered to be the final straw was when Haleef had seen kidnappings of little kids by American Special Forces Units so as to bring their parents out of hiding who were deemed terrorists.

This rubbed him wrong in the worst way. How in the hell can you kidnap a little kid, keep them away from all that they know, and have them scared to death without their parents or any idea of what is going on, just to capture someone you believe is against your political design?

In America, this would be considered "kidnapping for ransom" which could land you the death penalty.

He never understood how America could *themselves* commit a terrorist act in order *to* catch a terrorist. This shit made no sense.

Then, one day as they were leaving the base to get food supplies, they encountered two beautiful young Iraqi girls. They were playing and jumping rope in their front lawn having a great time.

Haleef had always thought that Middle Eastern Countries didn't have any grass. In all of the pictures he had seen, it was only comprised of sand.

So when he saw the two little girls playing in a yard full of beautiful green grass along with the overall sense of happiness in their faces and the entire scene before him, he began to wonder what else was a lie.

As he reflected, he did not remember a single killing or so called suicide bombing in the

Middle East by Middle Eastern themselves, that did not have a true moral principle behind it.

All of the American soldiers that had been killed on his deployment were actually the aggressors.

What people did not know was that suicide bombings were the only way to even the playing fields between the Americans and the Iraqi's.

For example, America had laser guided bombs that could blow up an entire Iraqi town, M-16's, body armor, robots, you name it. So it was impractical for Iraqi's to go toe to toe with such a force head on.

Americans also liked to break into Mosque's and private homes where they believed certain individuals were at 4 o'clock in the morning and kill everyone in the home. Even the small children.

So such cowardice could only be met with a design so unfamiliar and so subtle so as to be wholly unable for any force on earth to be prepared for.

The child suicide bomber.

It sounded harsh. But when you consider the fact that they would more than likely die *anyway* from a smart bomb, or gunfire from a military convoy while playing in the yard, it was very practical and goal-oriented.

So kids would often be strapped with enough explosives to level an entire football field and then pretend to beg for food, or casually ride a bike towards a group of soldiers and BOOOOM! They would all be killed.

This terrified America. They said that this was immoral. Yet kidnapping, raping and torture wasn't?

Iraqi's were simply trying to defend their land and their assets from intruders such as the United States Military.

They were brilliant. When the United States came for their oil and overwhelmed them by surprise, they set the oil wells on fire. They knew what these wars were about.

It made Washington look and feel like complete assholes for strategizing, lying to the American people, killing innocent men, women and children, all to have what they ultimately came for, utterly destroyed.

Haleef had told Wyreek a number of stories.

One in particular was when four men in his military unit jumped off the back of an armored vehicle and kidnapped two little girls.

Haleef, watched as it unfolded right before his eyes.

Kirk Wilberts, of the 116th regiment was the ring leader. In the fall of 92' Haleef witnessed Brigade General Kirk Wilberts jump from an armored vehicle and aim his M-16 rifle at the girls.

Simultaneously, three more men from his unit jumped from the truck with guns trained directly on the girls.

Haleef could not believe what he was seeing. Then, just as quickly as it started, the armored car that Haleef himself had been riding in the back of made a right turn down one of Bagdad's many side streets.

At that point Haleef could no longer see what was occurring. But he had seen enough.

The image of such young children hurt him so badly, later on that night he vowed to make amends.

What made his response so quick and deadly was the very next morning hearing a guy sitting beside him make macho jokes about how tight the two young *towel head* girls' pussy were and what he wanted to do to them tonight.

Haleef was so enraged that he could not eat or think properly.

Killing the four men responsible for the rape and kidnapping of those two beautiful girls became his every thought. An act such as this could not be justified. Ever.

Haleef excused himself from the table and went to the bathroom.

He looked in the mirror at himself. Calling his commander and telling him what he had overheard at the table might get him killed. The commander himself may be involved.

Haleef now understood that if he dared open his mouth without a more decisive action, whomever he told would do everything in their power to keep the incident on the hush and prevent the backlash that the American government would be sure to receive.

An act of this nature would most definitely tarnish the name of an already hated and questionable American government.

Haleef doused his face with cold water and prayed before exiting the bathroom.

It was now 4:30 a.m. His unit was scheduled to run the daily 2 miles in less than 15 minutes.

About 10 minutes later Haleef heard the all too familiar whistle blowing. He saw his commander come out first spitting wads of tobacco out of his mouth onto the ground.

"Get Youuuurrr   Asssses out here right now!!!!"

Groups of men in 3's and 4's came running out of the barracks sloppily putting on uniforms with cold still in their eyes.

Haleef just watched in disgust. He couldn't understand how every single day, seven days a week, the same protocol was followed, yet, none of them were ready. Alarm clocks were not set, teeth were not brushed, beds were not made and everyone appeared completely disoriented.

Then Kirk Wilberts, came out with three men following close behind. They appeared nervous.

Haleef knew that Kirk was definitely involved in the kidnapping as he had seen him with his own eyes.

Jeremy Trotter was right behind Kirk talking and gesturing his hands frantically.

As Haleef got closer, he could hear something to the effect that the girls were locked in one of the many port-a-potty's in the back of the barracks. There were twelve of them.

Haleef could barely hold his anger in when he had to stand by Kirk in formation. He wanted to punch him in the face right then and there.

But Haleef knew that it would be best to wait until the running began. Haleef had something for his ass.

When the whistle blew again everyone began running. Haleef followed closely behind the group of four which contained Kirk Wilberts and his three flunkies.

Haleef knew that the men would not be able to contain themselves for long and that it would drive them crazy leaving the girls that they had kidnapped completely unattended. There was also a chance that the commander would do random checks to ensure that none of his men were hiding out or on the phone talking to their girlfriends in one of the many port-a-pottys behind the barracks.

When the unit reached the bend which was situated halfway through the course, Haleef ran a bit quicker and right up on Kirk Wilberts. Kirk turned momentarily thinking that someone was trying to pass him in the formation that they had been running.

Suddenly someone had gripped his chin from behind. Kirk tried to pry the hand away while turning around but it was too late. He was dead before he hit the ground.

Haleef quickly bent over the body acting as if he were tending to a fallen group member. Eleven others ran right past without a second thought. They merely laughed or chuckled at what they believed to be one of their own who had sprang their ankle or passed out from exhaustion.

Haleef's heart was pounding rapidly. A natural desire to flee had kicked in. But Haleef knew that he could not abandon his post just yet.

Haleef ran as hard and fast as he could until he caught up with the last of the bunch. As he ran behind them, he knew that he had to somehow get to the girls locked in the port-a-potty's.

A count would be conducted before breakfast and Kirk would surely be sought after.

At the end of the trail, it was clear that no one even missed Kirk. They were all catching their breaths and trying to get themselves together.

Haleef looked over at the twelve port-a-potty's about 200 hundred yards from where they stood. He could not stop thinking about those poor little girls. He pictured them tied up, screaming, yelling and hoping to stay alive.

They had been kidnapped and stripped of their dignity.

Even adults that have been kidnapped in the past are known to have been traumatized for the rest of their lives and have recurring flashbacks of the ordeal.

But these girls were no older than 8 or 9 years old. They *had* to be terrified in that dark, unventilated, foul-smelling port-a-potty.

Haleef had to get to the girls. He had an idea.

"Uuuuh Sarge."

Haleef held his stomach and called to his Sergeant who was cleaning his weapons.

"What asshole." The Sergeant replied.
"Sarge. I have to shit. May I be excused?"

Haleef could have won an Emmy award for best actor.

"I don't care if you shit your guts out boy. You just make sure you are back for morning count."

Haleef answered.

"Yes sir."

Haleef walked the long distance to the port-a-potty's at a rapid pace but sure not to run.

When Haleef got to the first port-a-potty he opened the door.

It was empty.

He then went to the next one. It was empty also.

But this time he stepped in and closed the door. He had to make sure that he wasn't being watched. If he looked in all of the port-a-potties and someone saw this, this would immediately raise suspicion.

Haleef slowly cracked the door and peeked in the direction of the barracks a full 200 yards away. No one was paying him any attention.

Haleef opened the door and stepped out. He went to the next port-a-potty. Nothing. Then the next. Nothing. The next. Nothing.

Then Haleef heard it with his own ears before he opened the next door. It was the sound of two terrified little girls.

Haleef yanked the door open and was frozen in shock.

Both of the girls were crying hysterically and holding on to each other. Haleef opened the door wider and could see blood and feces on the girls' panties.

When the two young girls saw Haleef they immediately stopped crying. Sheer terror was on their faces.

Haleef stuck his hand out to whom he believed to be the oldest of the two girls. They were both crouched beside the toilet nearly wedged in between the port-a-potty's hard plastic walls and the foul smelling toilet filled with urine.

A tear fell from Haleef's face. He never thought that he would see anything like this in his life. He would rather death than such a sight.

The oldest girl finally accepted his hand. She was visibly shaking.

When Haleef began to reach out to give a hand to the younger of the two, the older one smacked away Haleef's hand.

It became clear that the older girl believed they were going to be raped again.

Haleef shook his head to gesture "No" hoping that such a gesture was universal.

He also said it aloud for good measure.

"No, I'm not here for that."

The older girl helped the younger girl up and quickly put her arms around her.

Haleef had to think quickly. He could not get too wrapped up in what was going on before him. He had just killed a man.

It was also a possibility that if he did not hurry up he would be seen removing these two girls from the port-a-potty. The two girls didn't even know English, let alone the ability properly articulate what had just happened to them or who did it.

Haleef held the two girls by the hands and looked the both of them in their eyes. He then kissed them gently on the cheek and recited *"La illaha illa Allah."*

He had learned this from listening to a few Muslim brothers at a community college in Newport News. It meant: *"There is no other God but Allah. May mercy be upon Us through Him alone."*

When this was recited the two girl's eyes lit up with some semblance of joy.

Haleef looked back towards the field where training was still going in the front of the barracks. Morning count was about to be conducted.

Haleef had to act now.

He suddenly grabbed both of the girls' hands and headed into the woods.

And thus began his hate for America and all that it stood for.

Wyreek never forgot this story. So because his uncle was essentially marked for death and in permanent hiding from the American government, he vowed to build a legitimate movement in his name.

Chapter 6

The Elder pressed a series of buttons on the large remote control causing a flat screen monitor by the fish tank to display a black baldheaded man.

He was in a room full of no less than 40 of his most trusted men. The Elder looked at one gentleman in particular when the screen fully zoomed in and came to a stop.

"This is of our first priority. I don't know who the hell he, is or who he works for. The only Intel we have on this man is that he is very articulate and that he is very deadly."

The Elder cleared his throat.

"Unhumm…This morning, a Newport News Commonwealth's Attorney that was on our hit list and scheduled to die next week was killed by our man."

About a month ago, The Elder had put hits on a combination of thirty-seven FBI agents, 12 ATF, and U.S counterintelligence agents working for the C.I.A that he had learned about through his contacts. They were a threat to his organization.

The Elder continued.

"He seems to represent the same force that we represent, although we have not formally brought him into the fold."

A brief smile went across The Elders face before he continued.

"Also, the assignment in Memphis that Amir, Wyreek and I were on last week was a complete success."

The room was quickly filled with handclaps and celebratory whistles.

The Elder continued.

"I just spoke to Amir outside. I didn't get the opportunity to ask him if he did in fact know who this black baldheaded man was because we have some company outside."

The Elders phone rang. It was brother Khalil, his Chief of Security.

Khalil was the first to spot the white Crown Victoria parked at the curb not too far from The Elder's hideaway.

The vehicle had been following his little brother Wyreek since earlier that morning. He noticed it right after the two of them had met up for a security briefing. He thought that he had left his cell phone charger in Wyreek's car.

So when Khalil made a U-turn and called Wyreek to tell him to stop at the next gas station he noticed the white Crown Victoria tailing the shit out of him.

Khalil did not like that shit.

All law enforcement in the Tidewater area were properly accounted for. Whomever this was, was violating the agreement.

When Wyreek picked up the phone he told him to get on the interstate and go straight to Jacksonville to see his uncle. No questions asked.

Wyreek complied.

Once Wyreek got on 95 South, the white Crown Victoria turned away and stopped tailing him.

Kahalil then himself tailed the white crown Victoria for about 3 hours until it finally got off on an exit in McClean, Virginia. Whomever it was, was NSA.

"Oh aiight you mutherfucker." Khalil said to himself when he saw the car take the exit. He had to place an order to have the driver of the car killed immediately.

So he called The Elder.

The Elder picked up on the second ring.

"Hold on Brother Khalil. I need to bring this meeting to a close."

The Elder put his hand over the receiver.

"Okay gentleman. I have to tend to this. Everybody be safe and keep in contact with your brothers."

Five minutes later the Elder gave Khalil the okay.

Chapter 7

Across the street from the mall, two forest green Chevy Tahoe's were parked side by side with the windows down. The occupants were waiting for a white Crown Victoria with a small brown spot near the left bumper to arrive at the mall.

The SUV's were within inches of each other but facing opposite directions. Then, in one quick motion, the SUV's abruptly sped off and pursued the white Crown Victoria as it approached the mall's main entrance.

As the white Crown Victoria looked for a parking spot, the two green SUV's got closer and closer.

Suddenly, an explosion of M-16 gunfire erupted and echoed throughout the parking lot. As the large bullets punched half-dollar sized holes into the vehicle, it appeared that the entire left side of the Crown Victoria was sinking into the concrete.

The occupant's body had been lifted from the driver's side of the vehicle onto the floor area of the passenger seat.

The driver's side door to the two Chevy Tahoe's opened in unison. Two men got out of the SUV's, opened the door to the white Crown Victoria that they had just riddled with bullets, and emptied about 30 more rounds into the occupant of the vehicle.

At first glance, the two men appeared to be decorated police officers or military personnel.

The first gentleman to exit was a short dark skinned gentleman in a grey Khaki suit exposing gold military assortments on his shoulders, signifying rank and position, possibly that of a major.

The second gentleman was much taller. He wore the same grey Khaki suit, but on his head was a neatly worn gray Kangol hat turned to the left covering a head full of dreadlocks.

The short dark skinned gentleman walked briskly back to one of the Tahoe's and pulled out a Polaroid camera from the back seat. He then jogged the few steps back to the white Crown Victoria and took 4 quick photos of the fat white man that now lay dead in a black NSA windbreaker.

The taller gentleman pulled out a small black Samsung flip-phone, dialed a number, and waited.

"We got him brother Khalil."

The entire incident lasted 28 seconds.

Chapter 8

"Why in the hell does he keep assigning us these high risk missions?" Tripp asked Leon.

Leon was drinking an Arizona Green Tea on his mother's porch in his basketball shorts when he got the call to hurry up and get dressed. Leon was Tripp's older brother. He was dangerous as a serpent, yet people slept on him because he had a baby face.

"I can't call it man. I just complete the missions and accept the paper. I hear what you are saying though lil' Bro. But we took that oath to do what we need to do to weaken all opposition and strengthen the movement."

Leon was the leader of the "Youth Squad" which consisted of the four deadliest brothers in the movement. They were all under eighteen.

At first, they didn't understand why the most serious missions were given to them. Then one day the Elder explained that he needed juveniles to do the most serious assignments because if they were caught, they would get lighter sentences and only serve juvenile time.

Tripp was 13. Leon was 16.

But this wasn't true. In recent years, prosecutors have been charging kids as young as 12 years old as adults.

Tripp had seen it happen too many times before. But he didn't have the courage to speak on it. In fact, he didn't even care of he was subjected to the death penalty itself. If it was for the movement, it was worth it.

But unbeknownst to either of them, The Elder did not pick them because they were young. He picked them because they were the most lethal and they were psychologically prepared.

The truth was, when men get older and wiser, they tend to think and rethink their actions. There was no room for this. When you were called upon you had to act. Right now. There was no thinking about picking your kids up from daycare, kissing your wife goodbye, thinking about your career or having any second thoughts about your life and morality.

Nah. You get the call and start walking to your car with your pistol. It's just as simple as that.

Leon and his little brother had killed at least 28 people in the last 9 months alone. And this didn't include those that died from the crossfire days later in or who now have shit bags.

At the moment, Tripp and Leon were being dispatched to the mall scene to pick up the body of an FBI agent who was killed in broad daylight by two members of the Movement.

Tripp was a little frustrated with this assignment because it seemed downright foolish to even attempt.

Here at was 10:00 a.m., the day before school started back up for the kids after the summer break and here they were going to pick up a dead body.

Everyone and their mother were at the mall last-minute shopping. Tripp was trying to figure out why of all days The Elder would pick today to kill a federal agent and then demand that he and his older brother get rid of the body in this manner.

It was suicide.

As he and his older brother got into the blue van which read *Paul's Construction* on the side in big yellow letters, he began to pray for the first time in his life.

Chapter 9

Special Agent Frederick Hustings sat quietly in a brand new 2014 Government issued Ford Explorer. He was parked near the front entrance of Patrick Village Apartments in the Denbigh Area of Newport News.

Agent Hustings was conducting surveillance of Latisha Wilson's second story apartment as part of a homicide investigation where an NSA was brutally murdered in front of a mall in broad daylight.

But even worse, the perpetrators then took the body away from the scene. So no body, no murder.

For this reason the NSA, CIA and FBI were working feverishly to locate the blue van that was said to have been the vehicle used to transport the body. For all they knew, the NSA agent could still be hanging on to life and in need of medical assistance.

Also, the public had no idea that the shooting involved an NSA agent. They only knew that a shooting occurred at the mall in broad daylight and that it was being investigated as top priority by multiple law enforcement agencies.

At the moment, the NSA was confiscating all outside surveillance and storefront footage in a 6 block radius.

None of the store owners themselves even had chance to review the footage.

Before it made the news, hundreds of agents went into every single retail store, gas station, and fast food restaurant within a predetermined area. They went straight to their computers and camera equipment. No questions were asked.

Now that the NSA had retrieved all possible digital footage of the incident, the FBI was assisting in locating those who may have witnessed the event with their own eyes. It was now a matter of National Security.

Agent Hustings sat and watched intently as a wave of beautiful women began their early morning routines.

While doing so, he reached into his top left breast pocket for a lighter and the half-smoked Newport cigarette he had sitting on the edge of his ashtray.

As he lit the cigarette and took a deep pull, he noticed a dark-skinned female walking to a dumpster not too far from his vehicle with a heavy black garbage bag in tote. She was wearing pink flip-flops, a white tank-top shirt, and a pair of baggy grey sweatpants.

But long after she had shut the dumpster and proceeded back to the building Agent Hustings was still staring at the beautiful young lady with his mouth wide open.

"Keep it together man. Keep it together. You have an assignment to do." He said to himself repeatedly.

Then suddenly, another woman much lighter in complexion slowly walked out of a building not too far from where the first female exited.

Agent Hustings reached into his blue folder for the photo of the witness he was supposed to interview.

He glanced from the picture to the woman about four times.

"Jackpot." It was Latisha Wilson.

The young woman was completely barefoot and had on a thin white t-shirt with a large faded Nike check inscribed on the front.

Every time she adjusted the heavy trash bag to her other shoulder her t-shirt rose up a little. Agent Hustings could see the lace print of her panties.

But her feet were ashy as hell.

Agent Hustings took a quick look at himself in the mirror and smiled. These girls were ghetto as hell.

He knew that he had a sensitive assignment and should be focusing more on the issue at hand. But he suddenly began to wonder if his FBI credentials would make him a lucky man this morning.

From experience, he knew how easily women submitted to authority, and especially his authority as a senior FBI Agent.

In his many years as an FBI agent, he had pretty much mastered the art of using his presence of authority to lure women into having sex with him. Indeed too many times to count.

"Fuck it" he said to himself. He had to speak to her anyway.

So he made his move.

Agent Hustings flicked the stale half-smoked cigarette out of the window and zipped up his FBI windbreaker.

As soon as the woman got to within inches of his SUV Agent Hustings abruptly opened the door and scared the poor girl half to death.

"Ma'am? Excuse me Ma'am. Young lady. May I speak with you for a moment?"

When the young woman saw the door open suddenly and an unfamiliar white man approaching her she took a swing at him.

"Hold on Mutherfucker! I don't know you. Back up!!"

She swung a haymaker once more for good measure nearly knocking him to the ground but he ducked away.

"Whoa whoa whoa… hold up sweetheart. I just need to ask you a few questions. Just please calm down okay?"

Agent Hustings reached into his front breast pocket for his FBI credentials.

"I'm with the FBI."

Agent Hustings stared into the woman's eyes giving her his most sincere look of professionalism and importance. He was full of shit.

"Unhum…is there any way I can speak to you somewhere privately? I promise this will take only a minute."

The young lady put her hands over her face as if she were about to start crying.

"God noooo! What has happened now?"

Agent Hustings could see that he young woman was about to start crying and getting hysterical. He really could not afford to be making a scene early in the morning.

"Hold on, just calm down sweetheart. This isn't anything personal regarding you. I would just prefer it to be done in private out of respect for you and your neighbors."

The young woman gave Agent Hustings a suspicious look and then began walking towards her building.

"And just what is this about officer?"

Agent Hustings took a few steps into the direction of the building the woman was seen leaving just minutes prior to him accosting her.

"This is in reference to the shooting that occurred yesterday morning at the mall."

He then reached into his coat pocket and pulled out a folded sheet of notebook paper.

"...I was informed that you work there at Victoria's Secret and may have seen something as you entered the mall."

The young woman wiped her face clear of the sweat and tears that had started to accumulate and slowly walked up the steps as if she were unsure if she lived there or not.

Nevertheless, she opened the second oak-colored door to the left.

"Come on up then, I guess."

Agent Hustings took three steps at a time until he reached the second floor landing. He quickly tucked the folded sheet of notebook paper back into his shirt pocket while smiling.

"Thanks sweetheart this will be quick I promise."

Upon entering the small apartment Agent Hustings sat on a stack of brown cardboard boxes in the corner of the living room. When he glanced to the right he was eye level with a purple vase that looked like it had been broken into a million pieces on at least fifty different occasions and then sloppily put back together with children's glue.

The shit belonged in the trash.

Agent Hustings looked around and thanked God that he did not sit on the piss-stained couch to his left.

Then the door behind him clicked shut.

The young woman stood there at the door with her back to it and gave Agent Hustings a curious look.

Agent Hustings had to break the ice somehow.

"Ok, uh, Ma'am…sweetheart…uh…"

The young woman cut him off.

"Aiyana. Aiyana Watson."

Agent Hustings gave her his brightest look of surprise. Latisha must have been so terrified that it didn't dawn on her that he clearly must have known her name to stop her and accuse her of working somewhere of which a homicide had occurred.

But people always thought that they could just lie to the police.

Agent Hustings laughed to himself and played along. Now he was in a position where he could blackmail the woman into giving him some pussy for lying to a federal agent.

But this was his ace in the hole. He would let her talk and talk and talk and then drop the bombshell when he had her right where he wanted her.

"My daughter's name is Aiyana." He lied.

Latisha appeared to relax a bit and headed towards the kitchen.

"Look, I don't have any of that healthy shit you probably drink."

Seconds later Agent Hustings could hear glasses clinging and clattering together.

Latisha yelled from the kitchen.

"But I do have some grape Kool-Aid, Agent uh...Mr. uh..." She tried to return the sarcasm.

"Hustings. It's Agent Hustings."

He could hear the refrigerator door open and then shut. Seconds later Latisha came walking in the living room with two huge glasses filled to the brim with purple Kool-Aid. From where he sat the cups looked dirty as hell. He scratched his chin in deep contemplation and reached for the glass with the least fingerprints on it.

"Thank you Aiyana. That was very nice of you."

Latisha sat on the pissy couch to his left with the dirty cup of Kool-Aid cradled in her small hands. When she flopped down on the couch he could smell the piss being released into the air from the cushions. But Latisha appeared utterly un-phased. She had a lot more than a pissy ass couch on her mind.

"Well let's cut to the chase. First and foremost Agent Hustings, if that really is your name. I don't know where you heard that I worked at that damn mall because that's bullshit."

She stopped and gritted on Agent Hustings as if she wanted to spit on him before she continued on.

"And plus, if you were doing an investigation and learned that I worked at the mall, you would've had my name already, which you clearly did not, because you had to ask me."

Latisha paused to give Agent Hustings a look of disgust as if to say "Yeah mutherfucker I just busted you".

"Then, on top of that, you dumb ass genius, since you didn't have a picture of me or my name or anything else to identify me, you had no real reason to stop me when I was taking out the trash

Latisha took a sip of the Kool-Aid.

So uh… let's start over shall we?"

Agent Hustings turned red and began to fidget with his hands. Unbeknownst to her this was part of his ploy.

"Okay. You got me. But there was no ill-intent okay? Trust me...I thought that well just maybe... I thought uh..."

Latisha cut him off.

"Look, how about you try by putting an end to all of the bullshit because it's not working. The cold honest truth is that you wanted some of this tight wet pussy right here didn't you? You saw this fat ass of mines when I was taking out that trash and now you are trying to play your little FBI card in card in order to get this pussy right?"

Agent Hustings turned redder than the Kool-Aid man himself.

"Well uh… not necessarily. You see…"

Latisha cut him off again. She felt the ball was in her court.

"Shut up, aint nobody tryna hear that sob ass story. You probably have never even touched or felt a black woman in your life have you?"

She was teasing.

Agent Hustings was stuck on stupid. He looked at the floor and then back up at Latisha.

At this point Latisha became emboldened. She began to think in her mind that it was fair game to tease this apparently vulnerable white man who was clearly out of his element.

Agent Hustings appeared completely shaken up. So Latisha had an idea.

Latisha stood up with a slight seductive look on her face and walked up close to Agent Hustings as he sat on the stacked boxes in the corner looking defeated.

After a brief moment of hesitation, Latisha reached down and rubbed on Agent Hustings chest and crotch area.

"So what's all of this talking for then huh?"

Latisha slowly raised her t-shirt up to her belly button and revealed a pair of light blue panties.

It appeared that Agent Hustings spirits were instantly boosted. He was grinning from ear to ear.

But Latisha was really trying to build her confidence. To her, this was a little harmless game of seduction. Shit, she might even get a few dollars for her rent just letting this desperate white man see a little flesh. But he was in her home and this was dangerous.

Latisha did everything in her power to maintain eye contact so that she would not appear shy. Or naïve.

But she needed some time to think a bit more. Maybe she could put something in his drink and rob him blind.

Latisha removed her hand from Agent Hustings crotch area and backed away a little bit.

"Wait hold up. Let me get myself together. Hold on a second."

But Agent Hustings wasn't letting up any. It felt like all of the blood in his entire body went to his crotch area.

As Latisha began to turn around and head to the back room, Agent Hustings abruptly stood up and grabbed her by the waist.

"Hold on baby girl. Where do you think you're going so fast?"

Agent Hustings was now holding Latisha so close to him that she could feel the budge in his pants.

Latisha became aware that this white man really and truly thought that he was going to get some pussy.

"Yeah right. In his fucking dreams." She said to herself.

"Look Agent Hustings you might as well stop now because…"

Agent Hustings cut her off.

"Because what *Latisha*?!"

All of the blood ran out of Latisha's face. How did he know her name?

Agent Hustings smiled to himself. This was going to be good.

"Why in the hell would a decorated FBI agent just randomly come to you and allege that you worked somewhere where a homicide occurred and ask to question you if they didn't already know your name?"

Latisha was at a loss for words.

Agent Hustings fed off of this with perfection.

"Have you ever done any fed time Latisha? Have you ever been charged with lying to a federal officer in a murder investigation?"

Agent Hustings walked up behind Latisha who had not even turned around since her real name was uttered.

"You asked me if I have ever felt a black woman before. Well, have you ever felt a white man before?"

Agent Hustings was now so close to Latisha that his dick was now pressing up against her ass.

Agent Hustings grabbed Latisha by the waist. He knew that she was in shock and absolutely anything could be done to her now.

Agent Hustings slowly reached down under Latisha's T-shirt and fondled her pussy from the back. He then slowly slid two of fingers inside of her.

Latisha gasped.

Agent Hustings unbuckled his pants and pulled out began to pull out his now fully erected penis.

He raised Latisha's shirt from the back and pulled down her panties. Latisha tried to tighten her vagina walls to make it impossible for him to enter her. But it was no use.

Agent Hustings rubbed the head of his dick on her pussy, and then, inch by inch, shoved himself into her.

Gradually Agent Hustings went deeper into Latisha. Once he had himself fully inside of her, he began to thrust his long penis into her as hard as he could.

Latisha held on to the wall and began to cry to herself.

A loud smacking sound of flesh pounding against flesh could be heard throughout the small apartment.

She was psychologically defenseless. She didn't know what to do.

"Ag…Agen…gent…Agent…Agent Hust…"

Agent Hustings was mercilessly pounding himself into her.

For a full fifteen minutes Agent Hustings had his way with Latisha. She just cried to herself and held onto the wall.

She could not believe what was happening to her.

Then suddenly, Latisha felt something shoot inside of her.

The deed was done.

Agent Hustings left his now softening penis inside of Latisha for another minute or so. He was savoring what he had just done. And Latisha was right. This was his first black woman.

When Agent Hustings pulled his long penis out of Latisha, she could feel Agent Hustings semen running down her legs.

She wanted to die.

Meanwhile, Agent Hustings had a big smile on his face.

Agent Hustings buckled his pants and kissed Latisha on the neck softly as if she had just willingly made love to him.

He then whispered into Latisha's ear.

"Maybe next time you won't lie to the Fed's huh?"

When Agent Hustings made this comment, for the very first time since he had said her real name she felt anger instead of overwhelming fear.

Latisha began to shake with rage. The only thing on her mind now was how she would kill him.

Agent Hustings wiped his forehead and looked out the window to see of his truck was still there.

Latisha couldn't believe this shit.

"Really?" She said to herself.

"Did he just rape me and turn around and nonchalantly look out the window?"

Latisha looked on the floor and noticed Agent Husting's gun on the next to his wallet.

His pants and his gun must have fallen to the floor during his disgraceful act.

Latisha slowly crouched low to the floor while agent Hustings looked out the window.

Without hesitation, Latisha grabbed the black and grey .45 Ruger from the floor, studied in momentarily...

BOOOM!!!!

Instantly, Latisha's face was covered in Agent Hustings blood, small fragments of his skull and whatever the hell else he had on his sick perverted mind before she blew his brains out.

Latisha dropped the gun and curled herself into a little ball on the floor. She rocked back and forth and cried in between her knees.

"Oh God." Latisha mumbled to herself over and over again.

Snot, spit, and tears ran down Latisha's beautiful brown face and gathered itself on the floor between her legs.

Chapter 10

It took a full 45 minutes for Latisha to sense the reality of what had just occurred.

Latisha walked into the bathroom and carefully unhooked each ring from a yellow shower curtain that her mother had given her two Christmas' ago. The shower curtain was ugly as hell but it matched her yellow toilet seat cushions and soap dispenser so she kept it.

While unhooking the shower curtain, Latisha made a vow to herself that every single move in her life from this point forward would be handled with precision.

No more room for errors.

Latisha quickly went back into the living room with the shower curtain draped over her shoulders. The living room still smelled of copper and gunpowder.

Latisha stepped over the dead agent and opened the window. The morning air quickly began to come through the living room dispersing the smell that was just minutes ago nearly unbearable.

Latisha placed the shower curtain over Agent Hustings body and headed to the kitchen. She needed some trash bags.

After locating the trash bags, Latisha stuck her small fingers into the box and pulled 4 bags out before tossing it back into the cabinet.

While walking back over to the body, Latisha carefully opened each of the four heavy duty trash bags. She snapped and popped each bag in the air so that they would open to their fullest capacity.

When she reached Agent Hustings dead body, Latisha got onto her hands and knees and proceeded to lift his legs into the first bag.

She then grabbed another large bag and began to stuff the top half of the body into the bag without lifting him off of the floor to do it.

When Latisha finished she was sweating profusely and had blood all over her from handling the body.

Latisha tied the bags to each other as best as she could and stood up. For ten minutes she wiped beads of sweat from her forehead.

She backed away from the lumpy trash bag in the middle of the living room floor and assessed her work.

The little nasty motherfucker looked like he was resting peacefully in a cocoon.

Latisha smiled to herself.

She now had to get rid of the agents White Ford Explorer parked out front.

Chapter 11

Had anyone been eavesdropping or listening to Latisha's repeated grunts and moans through the door they will have immediately assumed that she was taking a shit.

A real good shit too.

"Uggh…Uggh…" Came the loud grunts as she repeatedly tugged and pulled on the heavy trash bag.

Agent Hustings was one heavy motherfucker. He was every bit of the 230 pound cited on his I.D. Plus, another 30 pounds as Biggie Smalls warned us when a man dies.

It felt like the further she pulled and tugged on the bag, the further the door got.

After about thirty minutes of no real progress and nearly passing out from exhaustion, she gave up. She wished she had not installed that thick carpet in the living room last summer. Pulling the bag across the floor would have been much easier with the tiled floors she had originally.

Latisha flopped herself onto the pissy couch and glanced up at the wood framed clock above her television set.

It was now 1:26 p.m. "Damnit!" She yelled.

This morning's unexpected change of events caused her to forget that she had to be at work and clocked in by 3:00 p.m. Latisha was the evening shift supervisor in the electronics department at the Wal-Mart shopping center on Jefferson Avenue.

And although she had a full hour and a half to play with before heading to work, she would not dare play with it. Latisha did not have her own vehicle at the moment.

Latisha's license had been revoked nearly 8 months ago for reckless driving after being caught driving 75 mph in a 20 mph school zone.

Since then, transportation had become a major issue for her. She had become accustomed to riding the number 16 bus to work every day.

From a practical standpoint, not having a vehicle was inconvenient as hell. But financially it was cost effective. The bus only cost her a dollar.

But nothing was without flaw. With the bus, though cost effective, she often arrived at work either too damn late, or too damn early. Then, to make matters worse, the evening shift bus driver Ms. Collins was just plain disrespectful as hell. She would often ride right past Latisha if she was at the bus stop by herself.

This often led to unnecessary changes in her plans. When she missed the bus she would have to walk to Terrance's house or catch a cab.

And both of these options were entirely too expensive.

A single cab ride from Patrick Village Apartments to the Wal-Mart shopping center on Jefferson Avenue would cost her $26 one-way.

On the other hand, a ride from Terrence would cost Latisha her dignity, as Terrence often wanted some pussy for giving her a ride.

But these matters were altogether trivial in comparison to what she now faced at the moment.

Latisha thought about calling out today so she could handle her business and get rid of the body. But then she thought about this. Latisha had not missed a single day of work for the last sixteen months. Any subsequent investigation by the fed's or even the local police would easily uncover this glitch in her normal routine.

She also knew that leaving a dead body in her apartment while she went to work for 8 hours was completely out of the question.

Or was it?

On second thought, maybe that wouldn't be such a bad idea after all. In reality, the most pressing obstacle before her was Agent Husting's white SUV double-parked beside the dumpster which would immediately raise suspicion.

This left Latisha with only one choice: Ditch the SUV and carry her ass to work.

Chapter 12

Latisha quickly put on her blue Wal-Mart vest and jammed Agent Hustings keys to his white Ford Explorer into her front right pocket.

She did not have time to be cute. It was now 1:53 p.m. and she needed to be in the Electronics Department in a little over an hour.

Moreover, Latisha had not decided where she would abandon Agent Hustings White SUV.

Part of her indecisiveness was the fact that there were cameras all across Newport News and Hampton. At the stoplights. Store parking lots. Apartment complex entrances. Everywhere.

It would be extremely difficult to drive halfway across Newport News undetected. The SUV would in one way or another be spotted in a surveillance camera.

Latisha went into her room in search of the navy blue scarf that she used to protect her hair when she slept. She normally kept her hair braided and hated when her parts become fuzzy. After a long nights rest where she often tossed and turned a new hairdo would look like some shit.

Seconds later she found the scarf hanging on the knob of her panty drawer. But this wouldn't be enough.

Though Latisha was sexy as hell she had a big head and would most definitely need more than a scarf to cover it up.

Latisha cut off the television and locked the apartment door behind her. She now had a pretty good idea where she would abandon the SUV.

When Latisha exited the apartment building she looked like a stick up kid. And had it not been for her shapely figure and seductive walk, anyone who saw her will have thought that she was a dude.

Latisha quickly made her way towards the dumpster where the Agents white SUV was double-parked. There were still a few parents standing at the bus stop waiting for the A.M. kindergarteners to get out of school.

Other than that, there was no one in sight.

Latisha walked closer to the vehicle while pressing the unlock button on the set of keys in her hands. When she was about 10 feet away from the Ford Explorer she heard a series of simultaneous pops and clicks as the doors to the SUV unlocked in unison.

"Latisha!! Hey yo Latisha!! I know you hear me girl. Hey yo Latishaaaa!!"

Latisha was so focused on the task at hand, she had not heard her name being called. She simply swung open the driver's side door to the SUV and hopped in.

It came again.

"Hey yo Latishaaa!!"

Latisha's heart began to pound in her chest. She looked in the rearview mirror. Nothing. Then the side view mirror. Nothing.

"Latisha!"

Latisha then turned her body almost all the way around in the driver's seat and peered out the back window of the truck. She quickly directed her attention up towards the second floor window. It was Terrance.

"Oh hell no." She thought. She couldn't afford this shit right now.

So she sped off.

Chapter 13

Latisha realized that she had made her first mistake. Allowing Terrance to see her in the Agent's SUV was bad business.

Very bad business.

She was unsure if Terrance could hold water. If the authorities began an investigation and later questioned him about the vehicle, it could get ugly.

It also caused her great anxiety when she reflected upon Terrance's past. Terrance had a lot of run-in's with the law but always managed to wiggle free of the consequences while his friends often received lengthy prison sentences.

Latisha stopped at the light on Warwick Boulevard and flipped down the left turning signal with her index finger.

She decided to ditch the SUV in a wooded area on Industrial Park not too far from the train tracks. There were no stores on the entire stretch of road which decreased the likelihood that she would be spotted by storefront surveillance.

Latisha pulled the strings to her green hoodie as tightly as possible to conceal her face.

When the light finally decided to turn green, Latisha pulled the large SUV onto Warwick Boulevard and turned right. All of the jitters and paranoia which just moments earlier pervaded her entire being had begun to vanish with each passing second.

When Latisha reached Industrial Park Drive she made another quick right and continued straight ahead until she reached the densely wooded area she planned to ditch the Agent's SUV.

Bingo.

Latisha stopped the SUV and put it in park. There was trash scattered all about the small area.

Over to her left, by a tree that had been cut to a stump, was a rusted beach cruiser on two flats. It appeared to her that at some point a number of homeless people or crack heads had resided here.

She began to wonder if whether or not this spot was far enough away from the road. But after looking around a few more times she decided that it was perfect.

Before taking the keys out of the ignition, Latisha checked the side view mirrors to ensure herself once more that all was well and there were no stray crack heads roaming about the wooded area.

Latisha quickly glanced towards the radio at the green numbers emanating from the dashboards digital clock before stepping out into the wooded area.

It was now 2:09 p.m. Good timing she thought.

She loosened the strings to her hoodie and removed the blue scarf from the lower half of her face before stepping out.

Seconds later Latisha was headed down Industrial Park Drive to the bus stop on Jefferson Avenue on foot.

Chapter 14

Latisha was paranoid as hell. Every three or four steps Latisha had taken she glanced over her shoulder to see if she was being followed. In reality, it was impossible for anyone to creep up on her on this straight stretch of road. She would be able to both see and hear anyone coming in either direction well in advance.

Latisha's mind wandered during the walk. She worried about Terrance not being able to hold it together if questioned by police. Another concern was her nosey-ass neighbors seeing Agent Hustings enter her building and never leaving. But she doubted that anyone paid that much attention to the comings and goings of her building.

She had visions of K-9 units and federal agents rummaging through her apartment in search of Agent Hustings.

"Get yourself together girl". She repeatedly said to herself.

When the bus stop was in view she noticed about six people standing in front of Denbigh Trace Apartments waiting on the number seven bus to arrive.

Latisha dreaded the thought of having to stand at an unfamiliar bus stop. A lot of people in the city either knew her or was familiar with her face due to her working at Wal-Mart.

She always felt that it was a real risk being so widely recognized by people. A lot of customers believed that because they saw her at Wal-Mart they knew Latisha personally. People would often strike up the most intimate of conversations with her in public. Latisha would not have the slightest clue who they were or where she may have met them at.

When Latisha finally made it to the bus stop she only got a few nods from an older couple and stale cigarette smoke blown into her face by a group of teenagers.

She was invisible.

Five minutes later Latisha boarded the bus and was greeted with the ever-present rudeness and foul mouth of the evening shift bus driver Ms. Collins.

"Oh looky look. I see we like to just hop on any bus that we want to huh?"

Latisha ignored her but then managed to pull out the most wrinkled one dollar bill in all of the United States Treasury. Ms. Collins stared Latisha in the face the entire time and tapped on the large steering wheel while Latisha fidgeted with the wrinkled dollar bill.

After a full minute of trying to flatten the money, the device finally accepted it. The doors to the bus closed shut behind Latisha with a loud thump.

Latisha glanced at her pink G-Shock watch as she walked to the back of the bus.

It read 2:41 p.m.

"Good timing." She said to herself.

Chapter 15

Agent Gregory Mathis propped his huge foot on the torn leather stool in front of him. He had been waiting for the local magistrate judge so that he could present his second supporting affidavit for a search warrant. It was for Latisha Wilson's apartment.

He hated all of these new laws recently passed down by the United States Supreme Court. There was now a new law requiring all search warrants to come with a supporting affidavit detailing the reason for the search, and exactly what items were to be seized.

Back in the day, he and his partner Frederick Hustings would simply kick in a suspected drug dealers door, seize what needed to be seized and arrest who needed to be arrested with absolutely no problem.

Now, if he did such a thing he would probably lose his badge, his gun, and maybe even face a major lawsuit for damages.

So in a single day, Agent Mathis and his dayshift crew of federal agents went from being above the law, to being bound and gagged by it.

Every time he turned around there was a new policy or procedure that they had to abide by.

When Agent Mathis first became a federal agent he was always asked to show initiative and to be more aggressive as an undercover field agent. A lot of the other Agent's were soft and got stepped on. But that could get you killed. Especially in a city such as Newport News.

Agent Mathis looked at his watch. He'd been in the magistrate's office for 2 hours and 17 minutes.

"Fuck this." He said to himself as he got to his feet."

Agent Mathis headed for a side door and exited the courthouse.

"I'm going into that house warrant or not."

Chapter 16

As Agent Gregory Mathis sped through traffic he glanced at the official report of the at the mall shouting.

According to the report, authorities recovered 139 shell casings from the mall parking lot. 132 of them punctured the vehicle.

All 7.62 rounds. An Ak-47 most definitely.

Senior Special Agent Michael Dodson of the NSA could not have possibly survived such an assault. There was nearly 2 pints of blood in the front driver's seat of the white Crown Victoria alone.

139

But without the body or official confirmation that Agent Dodson he was indeed deceased, he was considered still alive. Instead, an abduction protocol had been put into effect.

Agent Mathis took another glimpse at the diagram of the scene. From the trajectory of the shots taken, it was evident that multiple shooters were involved.

"Great. Just fucking great." He shouted to himself as he weaved through traffic.

For all he knew, there could be a group of terrorists operating in Newport News right under his nose.

And the precision with which the attack had been carried out, the body of the Agent being moved, and the brazenness of it all, it could not be ruled out.

Agent Mathis turned left on Denbigh Boulevard. He was caught in traffic momentarily until he activated the blue emergency lights on his silver Grand Marquise.

He knew that he wasn't supposed to activate his emergency lights unless he was being dispatched to an emergency.

But he didn't care. This shit was urgent.

Chapter 17

Ms. Barnette sat in front of the muted television set with a recently purchased scratch-off ticket clasped in her hand.

She prayed that today was her lucky day. The $500 Jackpot on the scratch-off would pay her light bill and put a few extra dollars in her pockets for bingo tonight.

Scratch… Scratch….

"Damn!" Ms. Barnette mumbled under breath. She had lost once again.

She never had any luck with these tickets. Every single day for the last 42 years she played the lottery or purchased a scratch-off ticket. If she ever thought to save the money she spent on tickets she would probably be a millionaire by now.

Ms. Barnette's thoughts were suddenly interrupted when she heard a car door slam shut. This was out of the norm. Especially considering the fact that neither she, nor any of her next door neighbors had vehicles.

Ms. Barnette sat the losing scratch-off ticket on her coffee table and stood up. She needed to get a better view of the perpetrator who dared interrupt her afternoon of peace and quiet.

This was a special part of her day. All of the bad ass children in the neighborhood were at school and the neighborhood belonged to her.

When Ms. Barnette finally made it to the window, she was surprised to see a tall white man exiting a silver Grand Marquise.

Her first thought was that he was a bill collector or insurance agent. But the man had that look of not belonging. Of a man that was about to do something that he had absolutely no business doing.

At least that's what 63 year old Barnette Nicholson thought. And right now, that's all that mattered.

So when the tall white man entered the building and briskly walked up the steps she knew that something was terribly wrong. This white man was up to no good.

Seconds later, she heard the door above her open and then close.

She knew full well that Ms. Turner was at bible study. And Latisha, whom she used to watch when she was much younger, was no doubt at work at the Wal-Mart shopping center on Jefferson Avenue.

So she called the police.

The 911 operator picked up on the first ring.

"911 dispatch. What is your emergency?"

Ms. Barnette pressed the telephone to her ears.

"Yes, I want to report a burglary in progress…"

Chapter 18

"Freeze! Don't you fucking move damnit!!"

Four Newport News Police Officers burst through the front door aiming .9mm semiautomatic handguns in the face of Agent Gregory Mathis.

"I said freeze damnit!"

The Officers moved closer to him with their large guns still trained on his face.

"Don't…you…fucking…move!"

Two of the plainclothes officers from the Newport News Police Department's VICE squad jammed their pistols into Agents Mathis' face. The impact of steel upon bare flesh could be heard throughout the apartment.

And had Agent Mathis dared to move just a single inch from his current position, neither of the four plainclothes officers will have hesitated to blow his head off.

"I…said…don't…fucking…move!"

At this point the four plainclothes officers were pretty much just relieving stress and having a field day jamming their weapons into the white man's face.

Agent Mathis had not moved a single limb on his body since the four officers burst into the apartment with their guns drawn. But they managed to whip his ass nonetheless.

Master Sergeant Blake Reynolds of the Newport News Police Department was the first officer to enter the residence. Next, officer's Rodney Long, Dennis Chapman, and William McKinnley.

Minutes prior, dispatch had been given the description of a white male, mid 30's, about 6'1 and nearly 200 pounds who had broken into the home of a younger girl who was said to be at work at this hour.

After the mall shooting, all local, state, and federal officers were on edge and on high alert.

And a white man burglarizing a home in a predominantly black apartment complex was very suspicious.

Master Sergeant Blake Reynolds ordered Officer Chapman to handcuff the man.

"Chapman. Cuff him."

Officer Chapman quickly cuffed the white man and conducted a brief pat down search beginning at waist level.

As soon as Officer Chapman brushed across the waistband area of the white man, he immediately came upon Agent Mathis' sidearm concealed on his waistband.

"He has a weapon!"

Blake Reynolds and Officer Rodney Long simultaneously slammed the white man's face into the far wall causing blood to gush from the white man's mouth.

Agent Mathis could not believe this shit. Here he was, face down, bleeding from his mouth and his nose, and suspected of burglarizing a home. He had to clear this mess up.

"Just hold on fellas. We're on the same side here. I'm a federal ag…"

Officer Chapman wasn't trying to hear it. He kicked Agent Mathis in his groin as hard as he could.

Agent Mathis almost passed out from the impact.

Across the room from the mayhem, officer McKinnley was for the most part simply observing the scene around him. This wasn't the first time his partners brutally assaulted a suspect in their custody.

So while his comrades stomped and kicked and beat the living hell out of the suspect he silently checked out the apartment as he had been trained.

Officer McKinnley gazed from the deep freezer to the side wall beside where Agent Mathis was now lying face down in a pool of blood.

He glanced up at the ceiling and noticed what appeared to be pieces of human scalp and gray brain matter on the ceiling.

"Oh shit." He said to himself.

"Hey guys…" He finally managed to get out.

His partners were still whipping Agent Mathis' ass over in the opposite corner of the apartment.

He had to repeat himself.

"Hey guys!!! Cut it the fuck out!!! Listen!!!"

This finally got their attention.

Blake Reynolds walked over to officer McKinnley with an angered expression on his face. He acted as if his fellow officer had interrupted a passionate love making with his wife.

Sometimes roughing up suspects felt that good to him.

"What McKinnley? What is it?"

Officer McKinnley pointed at the blood splatters on the wall and ceiling. After a brief second, Master Sergeant Blake Reynolds quickly holstered his side arm and reached for his flashlight.

First, he shined his light upon the deep freezer.

Nothing.

Then the far wall.

There, he noticed small amounts high velocity blood splatter covering random parts of the wall.

Then the ceiling.

As Officer McKinnley walked a bit closer to inspect the walls and the ceiling he tripped over a huge black garbage bag. He had not the slightest idea what was in the bag, but his gut feelings as a cop of nine years suddenly kicked in.

Officer McKinnley nudged the bag with his foot. When he did so, he froze in position and all of the blood left his face.

"Oh shit. It's a body in here fellas."

Chapter 19

On the front page of every newspaper across the nation it read in big bold print: 'FBI AGENT CHARGED WITH BRUTALLY KILLING PARTNER".

ABC, CBS, CNN, NBC, and every other news station in the nation with 3 letters played scenes of federal agents removing items of evidence from Latisha's home and placing them in a mobile FBI command center positioned in front of her building.

They even considered her pissy ass couch as evidence.

When news spread about the shooting, Kathy, her heartless ass aunt, called asking about a purse that she had left there over 2 years ago. She only wanted to know if investigators had taken it.

Not one time did she ask if Latisha was Okay.

Meanwhile, police and federal investigators went door to door asking questions to any and every one who dared answer:

"Did you hear any shots?"

"Did you hear any screaming or arguing?"

"How long have you lived here?"

They mostly got a bunch of doors slammed in their faces.

Chapter 20

Agent Gregory Mathis paced the small cell back and forth like a caged lion. A scared, bitch-ass lion.

Less than 30 minutes after Agent Mathis had been caught in Latisha's apartment he had been booked into the Newport News City Jail.

He was charged with murdering a federal agent which was a Capital offense and which could get him the death penalty.

In his 16 years as an FBI agent he had put many people behind bars. But at no time did he ever stop to think about how any of these individuals may have felt in these little tiny cells.

157

He momentarily reflected on a number of suspects that he had planted drugs on when he was unable to catch them red-handed and needed a reason to justify an arrest to his superiors.

Had Agent Mathis known this was what people experienced in jail he would not have done half of the crooked shit that he had done to people over the years.

"These little cells will drive a man mad." He said to himself.

Agent Mathis hadn't even been in the cell for a full 20 minutes and he was already losing it.

The sheer isolation was tearing him apart.

"Fuck this," he thought. All he had to do was call headquarters and explain everything right? Wrong. He wasn't even supposed to be in the house anyway. He did not have a warrant nor did he have permission from his commander to deviate from procedure so as to be covered in a situation such as this.

He was fucked.

He had to call his wife and let her know what was going on.

"C.O! Hey C.O! Can I use the phone man? Hey yo C.O, I need to use the phone man!"

No one had passed his cell since last night when he was finally booked and processed. It was now 3:00 in the morning.

He most certainly wouldn't be getting a phone call at this hour.

Agent Mathis sat on the hard steel bunk and began to rock back and forth with his head cupped in his hands.

He began to sob and cry uncontrollably.

Like a little bitch.

Chapter 21

When Latisha got off of work she went to stay over her best friend Lauren's house. That was the least that Lauren could do under the circumstances.

Police had advised Latisha that her house was officially a homicide scene and that she would have to find a place to stay for at least the next few days while they investigated.

Latisha was questioned extensively both over the phone and in person. This had occurred a total of fifteen times in the course of just 12 hours.

The purpose of these interviews didn't make any sense to Latisha. According to police, they had an open and shut case. The Agent's partner, Agent Gregory Mathis was caught in her house when police arrived and the body was located.

When she learned this through her supervisor her heart pounded a million beats per second. She kept asking herself how in the fuck he got into her house in the first place.

Did he know? Did he come to arrest her? Was the agent wearing a wire and his partner was listening in?

Question after question after question popped into her head.

Also, one detective noted that there was no way that Agent Mathis had killed his partner and bagged him in the small amount time that it took for police to respond to the burglary call made just 3 minutes prior by a neighbor.

Something else bothered Latisha too. Officer Brandy Holmes, the lead investigator, repeatedly asked Latisha if she saw a white Ford Explorer.

When this question was asked, Officer Holmes appeared to have been searching Latisha's eyes for a lie.

But she successfully made it through all interrogations nonetheless.

The next morning, Latisha caught the bus to her house. Although her apartment was still being processed, she was still permitted to get some of her belongings. Police were mainly focused on the living room at the moment.

Police made Latisha wear a pair of what looked to be hair nets over her tennis shoes before stepping into her apartment.

One of the officers referred to the hairnet looking thing-a-majigs as "Booties". Booties were worn by police so that they would not contaminate the crime scene by tracking anything onto the scene that was not there before.

It was pure hell having to walk through her own apartment and see police rummaging through her personal belongings.

The female officer accompanying Latisha watched her as she gathered a few things to hold her over for the next few nights.

But she had to grab something that wasn't particularly legal.

Latisha glanced back at the female officer to see if the she was paying attention.

By the grace of God, the female officer had logged on to Facebook. Latisha quickly reached into her top drawer where a pearl handled .380 Smith & Wesson was stashed.

After tucking the small weapon into her waistband, Latisha quickly turned around towards the closet and grabbed an overnight bag that she had stashed in the corner of her closet.

When Latisha slung the overnight bag over her shoulders Officer Holmes finally glanced up and put her cell phone into her pocket.

Latisha addressed the female officer for the very first time.

"Uhh… Officer Holmes. Since they are still processing my apartment, where am I supposed to go tonight? Do they have anything set up for me to lay my head?"

Officer Holmes gave Latisha a half smile.

"Nope."

Chapter 22

Latisha could not believe this shit. How could they not provide her with a place to stay? It wasn't her fault that this nasty mutherfucker decided to rape her.

And though they didn't know this, they had who they believed to be the culprit. Latisha should have been in the clear at this point.

Latisha reached into her purse and grabbed her phone. She had to call her sister. Her sister would know what to do.

Three rings later Medina answered the phone.

"What's up little sis? You aiiight?"

Medina didn't watch the news. It only pissed her off. The media lied so much it was ridiculous to watch and take seriously.

This being the case, neither Medina nor Amir had a clue what was going on with Latisha or the dead FBI agent being found in her home.

As soon as Medina picked up the phone, Latisha began to talk very fast about what was going on and what she had done. Medina kept telling her not to talk over the phone and just wait until she and Amir came to pick her up.

Latisha complied.

Medina made her feel so much safer. She wished that they were still young and boys never became a part of either of their lives. This is when life was perfect.

But after that first kiss from a boy, other things besides family became the daily priority. They fell in love with knuckleheads and roughnecks. After that, it was all she wrote. The conversations ceased and the two sisters unwittingly grew apart.

As these thoughts raced through her head, Latisha spotted a large Burgundy Ford Excursion pull up to the curb where she stood.

Medina jumped out of the large SUV and ran to her little sister. They ran into each other's arms as if Latisha were being released from the enemy.

"Le-Leeeee!!"

"Me Meeeee."

They hugged each other for what seemed like an eternity.

"Don't worry little sis. I got you now."

Amir slowly got out of the large truck and opened the back passenger door. The two sisters needed to get reacquainted.

Chapter 23

Amir could not believe what he was hearing come out of Latisha's mouth. The more she said, the more it seemed surreal.

Amir had not known Latisha very well. He only knew what Medina had told him about the two of them growing up, and some of the things that they had gone through as children. After Amir and Medina had gotten married and moved to midtown, the two of them pretty much started doing their own thing.

Latisha had a boyfriend, Medina had a husband, and they grew apart unwittingly.

Amir got up from the couch and walked into the main part of the kitchen where the two sisters talked with tears streaming down their beautiful faces.

Prior to him sitting at the table he had been in the living room listening. He wasn't spying on them though. Both Latisha and Medina knew Amir was listening intently from the couch in the next room trying to understand what had happened.

But now Amir had a few questions.

Amir sat directly across the table from Latisha. Medina was seated to his right.

"Latisha. Did anybody, and I mean *anybody* see you get into to the Agents SUV?"

Latisha quickly answered.

"No. No, I don't think so."

Amir pulled his seat to the table a bit closer and peered into Latisha's soul.

"Latisha, I am going to ask you again. Did anybody see you in that vehicle?"

Latisha paused for a second and then looked down to the floor. Oh shit. Terrance.

"You know what Amir. Terrance saw me in the truck. He had called my name from his second story window but I pulled off on his ass."

Amir's eyes widened.

"Terrance?"

That named sounded familiar. Amir tapped on the table with his index finger a few times to try to bring back a recollection of this cat.

"Terrence Wilkerson? That bitch ass nigga from 9th street? Dark-skinned, skinny nigga?"

Latisha nodded her head *yes*.

"Yeah I know that rattin' ass nigga."

All three of them knew that Terrance was a rat. Nearly all of his homeboys were doing fed time.

When raids were conducted by the fed's, when indictments were handed down, and when everyone's properties were seized except for Terrance's, the whole hood knew what was up. He was snitching.

Amir always wondered why he was still alive.

Hassan and Kentrell, two of the twelve that had been indicted, had gotten out on bond and shot Terrance's mother's house up at least 7 times in two days. They wanted him dead no question.

And though Terrance never testified, the feds had evidence that only Terrance could have provided. So he was branded by the hood.

Amir stood up and stretched his arms while he thought of something. Terrence seeing Latisha in the dead agent's truck was a problem. Police will have most definitely asked the neighbors, including Terrance, if they saw a white SUV and who may have been driving it.

Amir sat back down at the table and stared at the salt shaker. It was a bad habit he was accustomed to when thinking about his next move.

He continued to stare at the salt shaker, he spoke to Latisha.

"Latisha, we need to get to that truck somehow and burn it. You made too many mistakes. Your DNA is all over that truck."

Medina stood up and walked over to Amir.

"Baby, please don't get involved. All we have to do is tell the police the truth. That agent came into my little sisters house and raped her

Amir. We are going to do the right thing this time."

Amir started laughing sarcastically.

"The truth? Tell the police the truth? That Le-Le was raped by an FBI agent? That she blew his brains out while he looked out of the window? That she hid his car in a wooded area? That she lied to police about what occurred after they asked her 37 times?"

Medina was upset.

"Amir, we can't keep killing people and running from the law our entire life! This shit is serious. We can't go against the feds Amir. They will burn our asses. We *have* to tell them the truth!"

Amir grabbed Medina by the arm gently and walked her to the sofa. He made sure that he was out of earshot of Latisha.

"Baby, you know that me and my brothers can handle this. Yes, it's risky. But if you and your sister think that yall can just go to the police and tell them the truth and walk out of there like they do in the movies, then you can start saving money for her commissary right now."

Amir didn't mean to say that. He could see that he had hurt Medina's feelings. But he was keeping it real.

He leaned over and gave Medina a gentle kiss on her forehead.

"I'm sorry boo. But you have to think clearly. Think in terms of what they have done to innocent people in the past when it comes to law enforcement. They charged Little Sintrell with Capital Murder for killing a police dog when he was 15 years old. He aint never coming home Medina. And guess what he did? He turned himself in."

Amir called for Latisha to come into the living room with them.

"Latisha."

Latisha came into the living room with tears in her eyes. Amir motioned for her to sit beside him on the couch.

"Latisha, I need you to take my truck and drive yourself to work today. You don't worry about shit. You just make sure your routine stays the same, that you do not talk on the telephone, and that you do not speak to the police under *any* circumstances. If they ask that you come down to the station you ask them if you are under arrest. If not, you keep it moving. You just act like this never happened and call me or Medina if you need anything."

Amir reached for a business card that was sitting on the coffee table in front on him.

"Here is my lawyer. His name is Aaron Williams. You are to produce this card to anyone who fucks with you without a warrant signed by a judge for your arrest. Do you hear me? "

Amir handed the business card to Latisha. He knew that Latisha had a lot of questions, but it was for her own good that she not know step by step how this would be handled by him. Women had a way of cracking under pressure. And even if they didn't, you would be so paranoid by the thought that they had somehow cracked that it was best to know that you yourself had not told them anything.

Latisha put the card in her bra and thanked him.

"Thank you Amir."

Medina was still crying. She knew that Amir would make what was going on with her sister a priority over all other things. Even himself.

Medina knew that this was the worst possible time for Amir to have to handle something like this. And something that had absolutely nothing to do with him on top of that.

Amir and Wyreek had just done God knows what, and here he was about to get involved in what could make him an accomplice to the murder of an FBI Agent.

Amir took his cell phone out his pocket and gave it to Latisha.

"Let this be the only phone that you use from this point forward Latisha. It is a secure line. Even still, do not talk about *anything* regarding what happened."

Amir held on to the phone for an extra second before letting it go.

"I mean it."

Chapter 24

Amir waited for Medina and Latisha to go sleep before he made the calls that he needed to make. First, he would call the elder. And not for help, but to let him know that he would be doing something that is not directly related to the movement.

He and his brothers had taken an oath and vowed to never do anything outside of the movement that could possibly jeopardize what they had built. After Amir got approval he would then be free to implement any and all resources that he had at his disposal.

Amir walked to the bedroom where both his wife and Latisha slept to retrieve a brand new phone that had never been used. It was a little bullshit Trac Phone that he had purchased when he was in Canada last year.

The Elder picked up the phone on the third ring.

"Peace God." The Elder greeted Amir.

"Peace Allah." Amir greeted back.

"What's today's mathematics God?" The Elder challenged him.

Amir was ready.

"Wisdom Understanding born out to Power."

"That's peace God. What's up?"

Amir wouldn't dare talk on the phone so he had to speak in a riddle.

"I need to buy some food from the store but I need to use your credit card. My money is kind of fucked up right now."

The Elder knew this to mean he needed approval to do something.

"Do you want me to order some take out so that you don't have to cook it yourself?"

This meant that he would give his full support to Amir and have his goons handle whatever it was so that Amir did not have to get his hands dirty.

Amir was needed in so many ways. He had the connect on the lawyers, he had a nonprofit organization that had the full support of nearly every politician in Washington DC, and he was a thinker. For these reasons, The Elder was very cautious about letting Amir do anything that had the potential to not only get Amir locked up, but tarnish his reputation in any way in the eyes of those that damn near ruled the nation.

Amir answered.

"Nah I need to cook it myself. It's for Medina. It's her sister's birthday tomorrow and I wanted to do something special. You know, bake a cake, buy a billion balloons, go bowling, shit like that."

The Elder laughed.

"Awww. Aint that cute. My boy baking cakes and shit. I know that girl loved you for a reason. But yeah, go ahead and use the credit card. And tell Medina's sister I said what's up and Happy Birthday."

Amir smiled to himself before answering.

"Will do. Peace Allah."

"Peace God"

Amir ended the call. He was now able to do what needed to be done. He had to hurry up though. Usually he sat around and brainstormed every conceivable possibility before he did something. But this truck needed to be burned and destroyed within minutes.

Amir got into his Burgundy Ford Excursion and headed towards Industrial Park Drive. Halfway there he started digging in his glove box for a lighter. He knew that he could go to the gas station and easily put gasoline in a gas can without suspicion. It was Monday night. Tuesdays he normally cut the grass anyway. So it worked out perfectly.

When Amir pulled up to the gas station he had a million thoughts going through his head. If the Agent raped her the way that Latisha described, then her DNA would be all on his penis and genitals without question.

"Damn."

Amir beat at the steering wheel as he got out. It seemed like problem after problem would surface if not handled immediately. He didn't have any contacts at the morgue to do away with a report or wipe the agent clean before testing.

Then it dawned on him. He *did* have a way to get to the body.

After going directly to the location where Latisha said she stashed the Agent SUV and burning it, he made a call.

Chapter 25

"Wait wait wait wait! Hold up. Did this mutherfucker really just say what I think he said?"

Cortez Roberts and Tyshawn Wilkins sat across the parking lot of the Dynasty Lounge on Warwick Boulevard in a rented Jeep Cherokee listening to the entire exchange between Aaron and the Russians.

And the situation was quite clear. Aaron Williams, head attorney at a major law firm in Newport News, Virginia, had represented Lovasco Ivashin, who just happened to be the youngest son of a Russian Mafia boss on charges of conspiracy to transport illegal firearms across international lines. He was also Amir's lawyer.

The government alleges that Lovasco Ivashin, and an unknown number of associates also residing in Russia, conspired to smuggle hundreds of thousands of fully automatics weapons into the United States.

Aaron Williams, Attorney at Law, had literally done everything conceivable to get Lovasco home. But it wasn't enough. Aaron Williams lost the trial and Lovasco Ivashin was subsequently given four life sentences.

So Mr. Pulintz Ivashin, whom is Lovasco's father and Mr. Izvanko Ivashin, Lovasco's younger brother wasn't too pleased about this.

Hence the kidnapping of Aaron's wife.

Aaron had been paid $1.5 million in cold hard cash to get Lovasco home only to disappoint the Russians. In return, the Russians then demanded that Aaron pay the $1.5 million back in full, which was why the three of them were there today meeting with the Russians in this manner.

So when the Russians refused the money, Aaron felt as if the air would not go into his lungs. He couldn't breathe.

"Nah, fuck the money asshole!" Exclaimed Izvanko, Lovasco's hot headed brother when Aaron attempted to hand him the bag full of money.

They wanted Lovasco home. It was just as simple as that.

Aaron walked back to the truck looking utterly defeated. His head was down and the huge Puma bag filled to the brim with the $1.5 million he'd broken his neck to re-earn in order to get his wife back was slung over his shoulders.

The Russians were playing for keeps. They didn't even want the money. They had other plans.

When Aaron finally made it to the driver's side of the truck he appeared to be in total shock. His eyes were vacant.

Cortez, from the passenger side, looked at his best friend and just shook his head before opening the door. He quickly stepped out of the truck and went to Aaron's side.

"Man, fuck this shit. We should just go in there and kill those Russian assholes. I'm sick and tired of this little cat and mouse game these cocksuckers are playing man."

Aaron actually considered just that. Instead, he dropped the heavy bag on the ground and glanced at his reflection in the dark tinted window of the truck.

"Nah, they have my wife man."

It looked like Aaron was about to break down but he managed to hold it together nonetheless.

Aaron motioned for Tyshawn to get out of the truck.

"I really appreciate you coming through on such short notice Tyshawn but we got it from here. If we need something we'll give you a holla."

Tyshawn hopped out of the truck and stuck his hands in his coat pockets. He looked his two closest friends in the eyes.

"Aiight, yall be careful though."

Tyshawn gave both Aaron and Cortez a quick handshake before heading to his own car across the street. On his way he glanced back to where Cortez and Aaron stood and pictured the three of them just going into the bar and killing everything that stood. He was that fed up.

In a strange way, he sort of admired the Russians. With them, it was never about money, nor were they cowards like the majority of the people he had run across in his lifetime. They lived by principle. Fuck the money. The Russians wanted their little brother back. End of story.

It also occurred to him that they would stop at nothing short of getting him back to where he belonged. Mother Russia.

They felt that Aaron could and should have done so much more to keep Lovasco from serving a prison sentence for the rest of his natural life. But it was all out of Dave's hands now.

Everything relied on Aaron's next move. And plus, it wasn't his wife to be calling shots. If he fucked up it could very well be the life or death of her.

Tyshawn got into his Tan Acura, made a right, and vanished down Warwick Boulevard.

Across the street Aaron grit his teeth together as hard as he could and kicked the huge bag of money with all of his might.
"Fuck! Fuuuck!!"

Cortez grabbed his arm.

"Calm down man. We'll get her back. Trust me. We just need to put our fucking heads together that's all."

Aaron looked up into the sky as he listened to his best friend. Had it been anyone else he probably would have punched them in the face and told them they could not possibly understand. But this was Cortez. His best friend.

"Yeah. Yeah you're right. I just need to get my head together."

Aaron reached down towards the bag. But Cortez stopped him.

"I got this. You just get in the truck so we can hurry up and get rolling."

While Cortez got the bag, Aaron jumped into the driver's side of the truck and slammed the door. He hit the trunk release button for Cortez and then lit up a wood-tip Black & Mild cigar while Cortez tossed the large bag into the back.

Seconds later, when Cortez got into the passenger side of the truck he immediately began to stare straight ahead with a stupid look on his face.

Aaron had taken notice that his best friends demeanor suddenly changed.

"What the hell is wrong with you?"

Cortez shook his head as if he were trying to rid himself of an image in his mind.

"I could've...I could've sworn I just saw somebody hunched over next to that dark Blue van talking into their shirt sleeve man. I must be tripping."

Suddenly, a black Grand Marquise came from the side of a building and into view less than 30 yards from where Aaron and Cortez sat in the truck.

The building had not been occupied for years. It used to be a Rack & Sack and was closed down about 12 years prior.

The Grand Marquise crept so slowly that an Asian woman walking into the Exxon gas station next door to pay for gas walked right past the car though it was still in motion.

Whoever was in the black Grand Marquise was clearly tailing the Russians. The vehicle had not become visible until immediately after the Russians walked into the Bar's entrance and were completely out of sight.

It was most likely FBI surveillance.

As the car got closer to where Aaron and Cortez sat parked Aaron naturally turned his head when the vehicle began to scour the parking and was directly behind them.

Cortez quickly reached over and tugged on Aarons arm.

"Nooo. Nooo. Don't look!! Just start the truck up and act like I never said anything. We might have a tail too, feel me?"

Aaron immediately understood. If the Russians were being tailed, it was possible that they were also being tailed.

As Aaron started the car up and began to exit the parking lot, Cortez reached to his hip and pulled out a black and grey Glock .40 from his waistband. It was already cocked with one in the chamber. This wasn't a movie where you had time to cock the gun before shooting like they did in the movies. Nah, in the hood, you didn't have enough time to cock shit. Especially in Newport News, Virginia.

Cortez sat the pistol on his lap and made sure that he kept the general area of the Grand Marquise at all times. If it moved in their direction or tried to pull them over he would empty all 17 hollow point bullets into the vehicle and its occupants.

After circling the block about 8 times, running red lights, and stopping at random stores to see if they were being followed, Aaron finally parked in front of a dike bitches house they knew from the hood named Kaylinie.

Kaylinie always kept good liquor and strippers at the house ready to strip and fuck whoever came through. And Kaylinie wasn't the type of dike bitch that cuffed her hoes. By no means. She would watch them get fucked, and then eat their pussy right afterward.

But she had three Cardinal Rules: You had to fuck them in the shower; you had to wear a condom; and you had to pay $375 for the pussy.

Aaron took the keys out of the ignition and addressed his best friend for the first time since leaving the Russians.

"Look, let's just grab us a few drinks and watch these little nasty whores shake their asses for a minute. We need to get our shit together."

When Cortez and Aaron stepped into the house, they greeted Kaylinie and two strippers sitting at the table rolling blunts.

Four more females were sitting on a couch butt naked taking shots of liquor with each other. Two more were on the floor eating each other's pussy. All of them were gorgeous.

Aaron glanced down at the floor again and suddenly recognized the woman on her back getting her pussy eaten. It was Deborah Falley from the Newport News City Jail. She was a Sheriff's Deputy that he had spoken to in passing while meeting with clients at the jail. He had no idea that she liked girls.

All he could think about was fucking her. Her legs were wide open. Wide, wide open. Deborah continued to moan and grip the carpet in her pleasure.

Aaron walked over to Cortez and pointed Deborah out. He explained that she was a Sheriff's Deputy at the City Jail and had no idea that she was a freak like that.

Cortez was a little more mature when it came to pussy though. He could see pussy and still think straight. Aaron on the other hand, even though he was married, would see pussy and lose focus completely.

When Aaron gave Cortez the scoop that Deborah worked at the jail, he grabbed Aaron by the shoulders and held him.

"Aaron, she works at the jail? The same jail that Lovasco is being held at? Newport News?"

Aaron, finally got the picture. This was God talking to him. Maybe he could work something out with Deborah. $1.5 million could work magic in anyone.

When the fiasco on the carpet ceased, Aaron pulled Deborah to the side and poured her a drink. She immediately recognized him as a lawyer that she had seen at the jail before and became tense.

"Nah sweetheart, I'm not here to judge. Kaylinie is my roll dawg. We are just here to have a good time."

Aaron talked to Deborah for about an hour. He found out where she lived, that she was from the Dominican Republic, that she liked the color blue and that her mother had just recently passed away.

But she seemed too unstable and naïve to pull off an escape of this nature. Deborah's lips were too loose and he did not want to get Kaylinie involved in any way.

He had an idea.

"Hey Deborah, one of my stick girls just got here from Atlanta. She has worked in corrections most her life. Do you think that you could put in a word for her at the jail?"

Deborah lit up with excitement.

"Boy, I can get a blind man a job   there. I know the Superintendent's wife *personally*."

Deborah put two fingers in front of her mouth and stuck her tongue through them seductively.

"She gets down too."

This was all Aaron needed to hear.

Aaron excused himself and went to the truck. As soon as the door closed, he pulled out a small sheet of paper and called Pulintz Ivashin, Lovasco's father.

He picked up on the first ring.

"What asshole?"

This was a rude way to pick up the phone but Aaron guessed it was well deserved under the circumstances.

"I have some good news. We need to speak in person."

Chapter 26

Hasita Ivashin, known only to her fellow Newport News Sheriff Deputies as Denise Watson, grabbed her radio off the table and headed to the elevators with a brown clipboard in her hands.

It was now 8:07 a.m. and just 23 minutes until Monday morning court calls. All inmates were required to be in booking by 8:30 a.m. for transport to court.

Denise got off the elevator and causally walked to cell block 6C. When she finally reached the steel door leading to the block she tapped on the door with her walkie-talkie.

"Okay fellas! When you hear your name come to the front for court call."

Hasita scratched her head before she began..

"Delonte Wilson, Derrell Boykins, Lovasco Ivashin, Matthew Craft, and Michael Ashcroft, come to the front."

Most of the men who were called wrinkled their faces and glanced around nervously at their fellow inmates as if to say, 'Man, I don't have a clue what's going on.'

Lying about court dates and acting surprised when your name was called is a telltale sign of snitching.

Neither of these individuals had court today.

Hasita opened the main door to the cell block and locked it back after all of the inmates entered the hallway.

"Okay, let's go gentleman, we don't have all day."

Hasita stopped and pointed at one of the men.

"Hey you. Yes *you* young man. Fix your jumpsuit and get yourself together. We can't have you in front of the judge looking like that."

Derrell Boykins did exactly what she asked and continued to follow her and the rest of the inmates towards the elevators.

Once the inmates were all inside the elevator and out of view of the cameras, Hasita pulled the fire alarm.

But it didn't go off. Instead, a white towel fell to the floor from the panel. Hasita picked up the towel and opened it. A large .40 caliber semi-automatic handgun was inside.

She then gave it to the inmate on her left.

Lovasco.

The rest of the inmates just stared straight ahead.

The elevator stopped and opened at the basement floor where the transport vans were located. Hasita used her ID card to open the basement level elevator door leading to the vans.

To her surprise, one of the Sheriff Deputies that had trained her was smoking a cigarette right beside the van.

When Hasita made eye contact with the other Deputy she knew that this was *not* going to go well for him.

Lovasco quickly aimed at the deputy and pulled the hair trigger of the .40 caliber semi-automatic handgun seven times in rapid succession.

The Deputy didn't stand a chance.

"Hurry uuuuppp!!" Lovasco exclaimed with a heavy Russian accent.

Immediately, Hasita and the three inmates bolted for the van.

One minutes and seventeen seconds later they were driving casually on interstate 664 East.

Hasita Ivashin and her twin brother Lovasco had perfected the first ever successful escape from the Newport News City Jail.

Chapter 27

Aaron Williams was excited as hell when he got confirmation of the escape. He knew that he was not completely off the hook as of yet. But as a small celebration, he opened a bottle of 151 Jamaican Rum and poured himself 4 shots.

Midway into the third shot, Aaron's phone rang.

He looked at his caller ID and noticed Amir's number. Amir and Aaron had not spoken in about 6 months. So to see Amir's number added to the sense of well-being.

Aaron and Amir went back about 12 years. Amir was one of his first cases appointed by the court when he began practicing law.

Amir had been charged with carjacking, shooting in an occupied dwelling, use of a firearm in the commission of a felony, underage possession of a firearm, and 14 counts of shooting at a police officer. Aaron beat them all. Well, all except the underage possession of a firearm. Amir did 90 days in juvenile detention and was put on an Outreach Program.

Everybody wondered how Amir beat it but Aaron knew. It was because in America it is rare that lawyers actually go to trial and fight the case. In 94% of all state criminal cases and 97% of all federal cases throughout the United States, defendants take a plea bargain.

With this being the case and it being so commonplace, when prosecutors are up against a real lawyer, they fold. They offer freedom. They dismiss cases. They suck dicks. Well, at least Samantha Hopson did.

Samantha Hopson was the Newport News Commonwealth's attorneys at the time of Amir's arrest and subsequent trial. At the preliminary hearing she expected Aaron to just sit there on his ass and do a piss poor job out of fear. She figured that as the lead Commonwealth's Attorney in Newport News, Aaron would not stand a chance by himself without co-counsel. He was fresh out of law school and appeared a bit nervous in a courtroom atmosphere by himself.

But three days before the preliminary hearing, Aaron Williams subpoenaed every last one of the police officers that Amir allegedly shot at and obtained video footage of the shooting.

Aaron did his thing at the hearing. Question after question after question he asked each officer.

"Were you wearing a uniform?"

"Did you announce yourself as police officers?

"Did you know that my client was a juvenile?

"And if so, why didn't you try to contact his parents when you finally got him into custody?"

"Did you question him?"

"Have you ever heard of the fruits of the poisonous tree doctrine?"

This was too much for the prosecutor. She looked utterly defeated at the end of the first two witnesses. Eleven more were to get on the stand.

But Samantha Dodson would have nothing of it.

"Your Honor, the Commonwealth requests a thirty minute recess."

Samantha Dodson approached Aaron in the hallway and asked if he was open to a plea. She said that if Amir pled guilty to underage possession of a firearm, she would drop the rest of the charges.

Aaron couldn't believe it. Amir was looking at a potential life sentence, 74 years to be exact, and here she was offering him 90 days in Juvenile Detention.

Aaron agreed.

"Okay, but only under one condition. You have to let me fuck you."

Samantha Dodson was so shocked, and yet, so turned on by such a brazen and bold statement, she blushed. They had been fucking every sense.

Now with Amir calling it brought back memories of the courtroom. Good ones.

"What's going Amir?"

Amir was excited likewise.

"Awww shit. Aint nothing big timer. How's everything been going with you? It's been a while."

Aaron paused momentarily.

"Well, for starters, I'm getting my wife back tonight."

Amir thought that he must have misunderstood him.

"Get your wife back?"

Aaron did not want Amir to get riled up so he kept it brief but to the point.

"Well, you know I screwed up on that case last year. So let's say, uh, she was collateral damage until things got better for my client feel me?"

Amir knew that he had taken a case with the Russians but he had no idea that his wife had been kidnapped.

"Damn Brah. I hope everything turns out aiight."

Aaron laughed.

"Oh it did. He made something like bond yesterday. Have you been reading the papers?"

When Amir said that he had not, Aaron filled him in.

"He fucking escaped! Can you believe it? Fucking escaped!"

Aaron had to play it off as best as he could. Hell, his phone could be tapped. Both his and Amir's.

Amir had not been watching the news. He made a mental note that he would start again.

Aaron knew that Amir didn't call for small talk.

"So what's up young blood?"

Amir needed to see him face the face to give him some of the specifics of what occurred regarding that dead agent and to warn him that Latisha may call.

"Aint shit. Me and a few of the brothers from around the way were going out bowling tonight and I thought that you and your wife may want to slide through. It's been a while since we got out."

Aaron had a lot going on. His wife was due back to the house at any second and he had to make up for lost time. It would be rude to just up and be doing shit the moment his wife was released. He needed to spend some quality time with his wife and console her emotionally. God knows what she went through for the last six weeks.

"I'll tell you what. You go ahead and enjoy yourself bowling tonight. When you finish, you and Medina come to the house and we will have dinner together. How does that sound?"

That was perfect.

"I like that Aaron. Take it easy."

"You do the same."

Chapter 28

Naomi Williams sat in the back of the van with a hood over her head. For the last 6 weeks she had been treated like royalty, though held against her will.

She had been in the care of Pulintz Ivashin's daughter, Hasita Ivashin.

The Russians made it clear to her daily that they were not going to kill her. And, she was able to talk to everyone in her family except Aaron. She ate the best food money could buy. She could use the internet. Watch television. She just could not leave.

Pulintz Ivashin, Lovasco's father, explained the entire ordeal to Naomi. She would be held for a maximum of 60 days. Not a day longer. She would be treated like a Queen. Not a finger would be laid on her.

He only wanted to get his son out of jail before he was transported to a federal prison. He felt that his own government would do something to his family if Lovasco did not return to Russian soon.

Russians were paranoid. Because of this, and because Pulintz was so well connected to Russian Organized Crime, it may be the thought of a select few in the Russian government that his son would rat to save his own skin, not knowing that he would simultaneously take down the entire Russian government in the process.

Unbeknownst to many across the world, Russia had always given their full support to organized crime syndicates that in some way helped to financially benefit Russia.

In any event, his son was no rat. Pulintz knew this. But his luck had been so bad lately, that if something were to occur in the Russian government contrary to their interests, it would appear that his son had indeed ratted the Russian government out. The timing itself would make it appear that way.

He didn't want this. For himself or his son.

Instead, he had to give Aaron some motivation to think outside of the box. He knew from witnessing it firsthand that Aaron did absolutely everything he could under the circumstances. Lovasco had actually gotten caught *in* a plane *with* 1,700 AK-47 rifles and 39 RPG's.

Pulintz had told he son over and over again, that when it appears easy, it is a trap. But he didn't listen. He made money hand over fist. $274, 000 a week to be exact.

So his father, Pulintz Ivashin and the Russian government, saw to it that he got his shipment of weapons weekly. They provided the cargo jet. They gave him radar jamming equipment. They provided him a pilot.

But Lovasco had been repeatedly told, "If you ever get caught, either you escape, or you kill yourself."

There were no other options.

Naomi also reflected on the time spent with Lovasco's sister, Hasita. All night they talked about saving the world from hunger, love, wanting to have kids, and the normal woman to woman chit chat.

Hasita had a look and a presence that radiated purpose. When Hasita expressed herself, her hands flailed in the air and her every statement was animated with life. Then, when she listened, she listened so intently and as if she made her own heart stop beating so as to not miss a single word that you uttered.

They went food shopping. Clothes shopping. Panty shopping. They played laser tag. They went out for drinks. You name it.

In fact, Naomi had the best time of her life with Hasita.

Hasita was special. She appeared to be touched by God. Delicate. Pure.

Time and time again, Hasita had given her a chance to escape, so as to show her that this entire ordeal was only about her brother. Not her. It was all love. That the Russians would not dare do any harm to her.

The only thing other than the actual kidnapping that was disconcerting to Naomi, was that on their way back to where she was being kept she had to be blindfolded. She could not know where the Russians were holed up at. It was too risky.

Then, eight days before the Russians planned to release her anyway, they received a call from Aaron. One of his stick girls, who went by the name of Kaylinie, had a girlfriend who worked at the Newport News City Jail.

Her name was Deborah Falley.

When Hasita learned that this Deborah knew, and slept with, the wife of Superintendent Tony Mills of the Newport News City Jail and that he did the actual hiring, this was all she needed to know.

Hasita didn't wait for her father to begin planning. Instead, Hasita walked to her father, kissed him on the cheek, and in Russian said to him, "This one is on me Papa."

Hasita quickly put her plan into motion.

Four days later, she was being trained at the Newport News City Jail as a floor officer.

Presently, Naomi was hooded up and put in a van.

Now free to go home, Naomi promised to keep in touch with Hasita.

But the two of them knew that this could not happen.

Epilogue

Aaron waited patiently for the phone to ring. The Russians had given him their word of honor that Naomi had been released and that she was on her way home to him.

Aaron had dealt with the Russians for a while now. He knew without question that when they gave him their word of honor, there was nothing else to think about.

But as each minute went by, Aaron began to wonder if something happened and the police picked Naomi up.

Naomi herself had done nothing wrong. But if the Russians slipped up during the abduction, or if they believed that the Russians were somehow involved in Lovacso's escape they would be on Naomi's ass like white on rice.

In fact, the FBI had been trying to nail the Russians since they arrived in America. But they couldn't fuck with them. They were too advanced in training for the elementary tactics of the American Federal government. It had been like this since the cold war.

Was their hideout being watched?

Aaron was losing his mind. All he could think about was Lovasco's escape, and that maybe police were watching Naomi thinking that Lovasco would try to contact his attorney, Aaron Williams, after the escape.

And if Lovasco got caught this time, he would definitely need a lawyer. A good one. A Newport News Sheriff's Deputy had been murdered during the escape.

Aaron began to get depressed. Naomi should have been home two hours ago.

Aaron walked back over to the bar area and grabbed a bottle of 151 Jamaican Rum. He didn't even bother getting a shot glass this time. He just took a swig without a second thought.

"Aaaahh."

He wiped his mouth and stared at his cell phone.

Click, click.

The front door to his house was being unlocked.

Aaron reached under the living room couch cushion and grabbed the Glock .40 that he had stashed there. He cocked it and headed for the door.

When Aaron got to the hallway area leading to the front door, he froze. It was his wife... Along with two Newport News Police Officers.

Aaron lowered the gun and put his left hand in between himself and the officers so as to motion for the police officers to stop.

Naomi brushed past the officers disrespectfully.

"Yeah, hold up bitch. We don't remember inviting you into our home." Naomi mumbled under her breath just loud enough so that they could hear.

Naomi then took a step into her house for the first time in 6 weeks. She slammed the door in the officer's face.

For about 30 seconds, Aaron and Naomi stared at each other without a word. Only after they heard the car door to the police cruiser close did they embrace.

Naomi suddenly broke down crying. Aaron held her close to him.

"It's okay baby. It's okay."

Aaron kissed his wife on the top of the head and continued to hold her. He knew that something wasn't right. There was no way that Naomi would waste one second getting home after such an ordeal.

A million questions ran through Aaron's head. He had no idea what had just happened.

"Did she go to police when she was released?"

"Did police follow her and think that she was involved in the escape?"

Aaron broke the silence.

"Baby, talk to me. What just happened?"

Naomi wiped her face.

"I don't know baby. When I was turning off of Woodcreek onto Dafney, I saw an unmarked police car parked in front of Ms. Tilerson's house..."

Naomi wiped her nose. Snot had begun to run down into her mouth.

"So I got out, walked right up to the car and scared the living shit out of them."

Aaron laughed, but did not say a word.

"I asked them what the fuck they were doing staking out my house like I was a goddamn criminal and that they needed to identify themselves."

Aaron held on to his wife's arm gently.

"Did they identify themselves baby?"

Naomi smiled.

"Hell yeah. I yanked out my phone and opened up the driver's side door like I was about to arrest *their* asses."

Naomi played the recording for him.

At first, all you could hear was the contents inside of Naomi's purse rattling around. Then, suddenly, Naomi's voice was heard on the recording.

"Uhh…excuse me. Do we have a muthafuckin' problem here officers? Are yall looking for something in particular?"

A Navy Blue Chevy Impala suddenly appeared on the screen. The screen was shaky as hell.

Naomi's walked closer to the vehicle.

"You know what? Get fuck out of the car!"

Naomi was then seen yanking the door open to Blue Chevy Impala like it was her own kids trying to steal their parent's vehicle for the first time.

Aaron was now laughing so hard he could barely breathe. But he continued to watch.

Naomi now had the camera trained on the driver.

"I'm going to ask you one more fucking time. What the fuck are yall doing in front of my goddamn hoooouse!!!"

When the officer began to explain she cut him off.

"You know what. Shut up. Just shut the fuck up and identify yourselves."

And they did just that.

"I'm Officer David Wesley and this is my partner…"

Naomi cut him off.

"Shut uupppp! He can fucking identify himself!!"

The other officer looked at his partner as if to say "Hey this bitch is crazy". But he answered her.

"I'm, I'm, Officer Travis Daniels."

Naomi began walking up the driveway and then stopped.

"Come onnn! Yall bring yall's asses on. Yall wanted to peek into my house so bad."

Naomi took a step towards the Officer as if she dared him to deny the request.

The other officer timidly got out of the car and began to walk towards Naomi.

This is when Naomi put the phone back into her purse and reached for the keys to the house.

Aaron was still laughing and holding Naomi close to him. He loved this woman so much. Underneath all of that discipline and sophistication as a Psychoanalyst at Hampton University, she had some gangster in her.

After they finished watching the video they sat and talked for hours. Naomi never mentioned anything about the abduction. Not once.

Finally, Aaron gathered enough courage to ask her.

"Baby tell me what happened for the last six weeks. You know you are my heartbeat.   I like to have died when they took you away from me."

Upon this question being asked, Naomi looked out of the window with the faraway stare of someone deeply entranced.

"Actually baby, it was one of the best learning experiences that I have had in my entire life."

She then told Aaron detail for detail about her encounter with the Russians.

... A Different Type of Enemy...

After an urban non-profit organization designed to protect the inner city youth from corrupted police officers becomes successful by two young men, every attempt is made by the United States government to destroy this organization as well as its reputation.

But when Haleef, learns of the goverments plot against his nephew and his best friend, he goes all out to protect his nephew and his organization.

...and *all* of those involved will pay with their lives.